DEATH STRIKE

Tyndale House books by Tim LaHaye and Jerry B. Jenkins

The Left Behind series
Left Behind
Tribulation Force
Nicolae
Soul Harvest
Apollyon
Assassins
The Indwelling—available spring 2000

Left Behind: The Kids
#1: The Vanishings
#2: Second Chance
#3: Through the Flames
#4: Facing the Future
#5: Nicolae High
#6: The Underground
#7: Busted!
#8: Death Strike

Tyndale House books by Tim LaHaye
Are We Living in the End Times?
How to Be Happy though Married
Spirit-Controlled Temperament
Transformed Temperaments
Why You Act the Way You Do

Tyndale House books by Jerry Jenkins
And Then Came You
As You Leave Home
Still the One

Death Strike

LEFT BEHIND™

>THE KIDS<

Jerry B. Jenkins

Tim LaHaye

WITH CHRIS FABRY

**TYNDALE
KIDS**

TYNDALE HOUSE PUBLISHERS, INC.
WHEATON, ILLINOIS

Visit Tyndale's exciting Web site at www.tyndale.com

Discover the latest Left Behind news at www.leftbehind.com

Published in association with the literary agency of Alive Communications, Inc., 1465 Kelly Johnson Blvd., Suite 320, Colorado Springs, CO 80920.

Edited by Curtis H. C. Lundgren

Designed by Jenny Destree

ISBN 0-8423-4328-8

Printed in the United States of America

06   05   04   03   02   01   00
9   8   7   6   5   4   3   2   1

To Shannon

TABLE OF CONTENTS

What's Gone On Before

JUDD Thompson Jr. and his friends are involved in the adventure of a lifetime. The global vanishings have left them alone.

After helping to publish several editions of an underground newspaper that explains what happened, Vicki Byrne, a freshman at Nicolae Carpathia High School, is sent to a detention facility, then to a foster family. There, she becomes friends with a Jewish believer, Chaya Stein, who has been disowned by her parents. Vicki leaves, knowing they won't want her either, now that she has befriended Chaya.

Everyone is aghast when their supposed enemy, Coach Handlesman, is unmasked as a Christian.

Judd accompanies Pastor Bruce Barnes to Israel and is arrested when he returns. But

Sergeant Thomas Fogarty of Chicago helps the kids and destroys evidence that would sink the Young Tribulation Force.

Vicki is caught and sent back to the detention center.

Now the kids face an uncertain future as their world spins out of control.

ONE

Danger in the Cafeteria

VICKI Byrne saw the flash. *A knife*, she thought. Her friend Janie turned and screamed as a girl approached with the crude object.

"I'm sorry, Darla," Janie whined. "I'll get you the stuff today. Tomorrow at the latest."

"You won't be gettin' me anything," Darla snarled. "You're goin' down."

Janie scooted under the lunch table and out the other side. Now only Vicki separated Janie from harm.

"I got no problem with you, Byrne. Outta the way."

Janie hunkered down behind Vicki. She knew the damage a homemade shank could do.

"I don't have a problem with you either, Darla," Vicki said. "Put that away. We can settle this without anybody getting hurt."

"I said I'd make her pay if she stiffed me again."

Vicki looked for a guard. Darla had waited for the right moment to bring out the knife.

"I didn't stiff you!"

"Shut up, Janie," Vicki said. She turned to Darla. "What if she gives your money back? Then everything's square, right?"

Janie tapped on Vicki's shoulder and whispered, "I don't have it."

"That's it," Darla yelled, pushing past Vicki and lunging toward Janie.

Vicki grabbed Darla's arm and pulled her down as a sharp pain invaded Vicki's side. Someone screamed. A whistle blew. Shouting. People crowded around, looking at her. A guard pushed people away.

"She's bleeding!" Janie yelled.

Vicki felt woozy. The room spun. Something warm ran from her side. The guard shouted, "Leave the knife in! You'll do more damage if you take it out!"

🌿

Judd passed the security gauntlet at Nicolae High. There were more Global Community guards this year. Mrs. Jenness, the principal, kept watch at the front.

Judd had vowed to become valedictorian

2

of his class. Speeches he had heard during the most tumultuous year in history left him hollow. If he had the chance, he would use the opportunity to give a speech his classmates and their parents would never forget.

Judd had never had to work for good grades. But his newfound faith had encouraged him to study the Bible like never before, and the discipline helped in other areas. Before the disappearances, several students had been ahead of him academically. Many of them had vanished. The rest he could pass with straight A's. He set his mind toward the goal.

But Judd had problems. His father's money was quickly running out. The monthly bills, the trip to Israel, and the expense of the *Underground* had drained the account. If he didn't come up with an answer soon, he would be forced to sell the house.

Throughout the summer, Judd and the others had written Vicki. When she wrote back, she seemed hopeful, but Judd could read between the lines. Northside Detention Center was an awful place. Pastor Bruce Barnes told Judd and the others to keep praying. He was working on a plan.

Between his many trips overseas, Bruce had put the Young Tribulation Force through a rigorous discipleship program. Ryan called it Bible Boot Camp. Judd couldn't believe how much they were growing and learning. And it was fun. Each new insight and memorized verse made him feel stronger. He had once seen the Bible as difficult to understand. Now each passage was a challenge, a truth waiting to be uncovered.

When Bruce was away, Chloe Steele took them through their daily paces of study and memorization. Her friendship had meant a lot to Lionel and Ryan as well. Nothing could stop the pain of losing Vicki. They had no idea when or if she would ever return.

"Thompson, in my office," Mrs. Jenness said. "Now!"

The last time the two had been face-to-face, Judd was in a police station under suspicion for involvement with the *Underground*.

As soon as Judd was seated, Principal Jenness said, "Your friend, Coach Handlesman, is continuing his reeducation with the Global Community. He probably won't be back. At least not here."

"What does that have to do with me, ma'am?" Judd said.

"If the coach really was behind the underground newspaper as he claimed, that little problem should disappear."

"And what does that have to do with me?" Judd said without blinking.

"Maybe nothing," she said, studying him. "Just listen carefully during the assembly. The new directives from the Global Community apply doubly to you."

✳

Vicki awoke to searing pain and cried out.

"Lie still and I'll get you something," the nurse said.

Blood stained the sheets. A bandage stretched across her wound. Vicki was afraid to look at it.

"You're lucky," the nurse said. "Didn't hit any vitals. But we had to stitch you up and give you a shot for infection. That was a pretty rusty shank."

The nurse left as Mrs. Weems came in the room. She was a large woman whose presence was felt anywhere she went.

"Care to tell me your side?" Mrs. Weems said.

"I'm fine, thank you," Vicki said.

Mrs. Weems snarled, "You're a strange kid, Byrne. You're different."

"Thank you," Vicki said.

"I hate different. To survive here you have to learn to get along."

"That's what I was doing," Vicki said. She explained what had happened.

"That was Janie's last chance," Mrs. Weems said.

"She didn't do anything."

"She was selling drugs," Mrs. Weems said. "She'll be shipped downstate to an adult facility."

Vicki had heard the hard juvenile cases were being treated as adults, but she didn't want to believe it.

"And me?"

"Come to my office as soon as you can move. I have some papers that need to be signed."

"Papers?" Vicki said.

"When you can walk, you're out of here."

"I'm going downstate too?" Vicki said, but Mrs. Weems was already out the door.

✳

The fieldhouse was full. Incoming freshmen were required to sit in the front. Most hung on Mrs. Jenness's every word. Several times Lionel turned around and looked at Judd. Lionel rolled his eyes each time. Mrs. Jenness welcomed students and introduced key faculty members. To her right were Global Community guards in uniform.

"Looks like they're stepping up security," John whispered.

"Why do they need eight guards?" Mark said.

"It is our hope," Mrs. Jenness said, "that when you look back at Nicolae Carpathia High School twenty years from now, you will think of a time of unprecedented peace and learning."

In six years, I won't be thinking about this place at all, Judd thought.

"Last year a faculty member caused great anxiety on this campus," Mrs. Jenness said. "He is no longer with us. We are grateful that the Global Community peacekeeping forces have been given the power to enforce the new rules."

Mark caught Judd's eye. "Sounds like trouble," he said.

"Belief is a private matter. Individuals must come to their own conclusions. Our new policies include zero tolerance for those who push their beliefs on others. Any student, faculty member, or other employee doing this will suffer quick and severe punishment."

Judd saw several freshmen look at each other. They had to wonder what Mrs. Jenness was talking about.

"Students will be expelled, their records destroyed. Hopes for higher education will be lost. Those involved in any divisive activity like last year may be sent to a Global Community reeducation facility."

John leaned over and whispered, "Are these just threats?"

"See all the extra cameras in the hallway?" Judd said.

A freshman raised a hand. Mrs. Jenness shook her head. "We'll save time for questions. Now I want you to see another move toward school unity."

Two students, a boy and a girl, walked on stage and stood by the podium. The boy wore black pants and a gray shirt. The girl wore a black skirt and a gray top. On the left shoulder of both shirts was a dove, the new mascot of the school.

"I liked it better when we were the Prospect Knights," John said. "It's hard to root for a football team called the Doves."

Judd stifled a laugh.

"Beginning tomorrow," Mrs. Jenness continued, "you may purchase these uniforms in the school bookstore. Those who object to our symbol of peace may opt to wear this." She held up the same style of shirt, but in place of the dove was a huge red *X*.

Vicki winced with each step, but she had to know what Mrs. Weems was talking about. Blood oozed from her wound as she made it to the office.

"You should have listened to me," Mrs. Weems said. "You shouldn't have run away from the foster family."

"I didn't," Vicki said. "When I became friends with their disowned daughter, I knew they wouldn't let me stay."

Mrs. Weems leveled her eyes at Vicki. "Everyone in here is as innocent as Anne of Green Gables. Learn from this, Byrne. Don't get sent back here a third time."

Mrs. Weems shoved a stack of papers toward her. "Sign."

"What are these?"

"Adoption papers."

"What?"

"It's your choice. If you'd rather stay here—"

"No," Vicki said. "I'll sign, but—"

"You want to know where you're going?"

"Exactly."

"You'll find out tomorrow."

TWO

Chosen

JUDD, John, and Mark debated the insignia that evening. John believed they should play it safe. "Once you wear anything other than the dove," he said, "you're a target. You can kiss the *Underground* goodbye."

"Not if every Christian takes the *X*," Mark said.

"At some point we have to stand up for what we believe," Judd said. "We've been skulking in the background, hoping we don't get caught. It's time to let our light shine."

John shook his head. "You'd rather play martyr than keep spreading the Word behind the scenes?"

"You guys are lucky," Ryan said. "At least you have a choice. We have to wear the dove."

Shelly arrived wearing the new uniform.

"They let everyone who works in the office take one so we can wear it tomorrow." Shelly had removed the *X* from her shirt and rotated it a few degrees. It now looked more like a cross.

"Cool," Ryan said.

"Mrs. Jenness will have a fit," John said.

"Yeah," Mark said. "Can you fix mine that way, Shelly?"

* * *

Vicki slept fitfully and awoke bruised and sore. She skipped breakfast and skimmed magazines outside Mrs. Weems's office, but she couldn't concentrate. She would go home with someone that day, and she had no idea who or where.

Finally, Mrs. Weems's secretary ushered Vicki into a small conference room. Vicki paced until the door opened. Pastor Bruce. She was so happy to see him she hugged him despite the pain.

"You're hurt," Bruce said. "What happened?"

Vicki explained. Bruce shook his head. She was gaunt. The more he heard, the madder he became.

"I've seen animals treated better," he said.

"Mrs. Weems said someone was adopting me. Is it somebody from church?"

"Yes."

"I can't believe it," Vicki said. "Did you talk someone into it?"

"Sort of."

"Who is it?"

"I'm not sure you'll want to go with him," Bruce said. "He's a bit of a disciplinarian. Stodgy."

"If he's your friend and from the church, I won't mind. Who is it?"

"Me."

"You're kidding, right?"

"I wouldn't kid about that. With the great need, they've relaxed the requirements. I got the go-ahead yesterday."

Vicki wiped her eyes. Bruce's sacrifice overwhelmed her. She had felt abandoned. Now she had a home again.

Bruce broke the silence. "You'll stay at my house. I'm at the church most nights or traveling. You can take your pick of rooms upstairs or down, but you won't be alone."

"I can take care of myself," Vicki said.

"I know. But I figured you'd need someone to keep you company. Get your stuff."

"Wait," Vicki said. "Janie!"

"Who?"

Vicki told Bruce about her. "There's just something about her I can't shake," she said.

"Maybe Janie is what I'd be if God hadn't found me."

While Bruce met with Mrs. Weems, Vicki found Janie.

"I'm happy for you," Janie said. "I'm going downstate, and they're going to throw away the key."

"Don't give up hope, Janie. God can help you if you'll let him."

"Save your breath, Byrne. God has a hard enough time keeping his eye on girls like you."

Judd came to Bruce's window when Ryan shouted. Bruce pulled into his driveway, and the Young Tribulation Force waited at the door. Phoenix had balloons tied to his collar. A huge banner on the garage welcomed Vicki home. Shelly ran out first, then Lionel and Ryan. Judd waited with Mark and John until she came into the house.

"I can't believe you're really back," Judd said as he stretched out a hand. "It's good to see you."

Vicki shook it firmly. Judd felt awkward, like he should have done something more than a handshake. He was glad when Vicki was distracted by the girl behind him. Vicki squealed with delight.

"This is the surprise," Bruce said. "Meet the newest member of the Young Trib Force."

"Chaya!"

Chaya had quit her job in Chicago and moved to Mount Prospect when Bruce offered her an assistant's position working with him and Chloe Steele. Vicki and Chaya would stay together in Bruce's house.

When everyone settled down, Bruce said, "The house-church movement is exploding, and there are many more areas to reach. Someday such groups will be outlawed. I have to work quickly.

"The 144,000 Jewish evangelists are all over the world, infiltrating colleges and universities and workplaces. People are hearing the truth. Satan is working overtime, too."

"It's hard to watch the news," Chaya said. "Theft and violence are everywhere."

"And not just that," John said. "There's a lot of white collar crime, too."

"People are stealing shirts?" Ryan said.

"No," John laughed. "It means business-people stealing things with technology. Hackers breaking into bank computers and wiping out accounts of people who have vanished."

Judd felt sick to his stomach. That must

have been what happened to his father's account.

"The enemy thinks we'll retreat," Bruce continued. "We can't. I'm going back to Israel next week for the temple dedication, and I'm taking Judd with me."

"How come he always gets to go?" Ryan said. "I want a chance."

"I hope you'll get one," Bruce said. "But not this time."

Bruce excused himself to get back to the church to prepare for Sunday.

"I have something to say," Judd said after Bruce was gone. He explained the money situation. If they scrimped and a few of them got part-time jobs, they might be able to last a few months, maybe even till the end of the school year.

"Tell Bruce," Lionel said. "He'd give you the money."

Judd shook his head. "We have to do this ourselves."

"Why don't you go to the bank and see if the account's been hacked?" John said.

"Because they might freeze the account when they find out my dad is gone. We need what little is left."

John said, "It doesn't seem right to let the weasels get away with your dad's money."

"Do you have enough money for the trip?" Vicki said.

"Barely."

"Use it and go," she said. "God will take care of us."

"Yeah," Mark said. "Exercise your faith. You've been depending on your dad's bank account."

※

One week later at the reopening celebration in Jerusalem, Judd and Bruce stood shoulder to shoulder with thousands who looked on from the Temple Mount. The temple was everything planners said it would be. And more. Nicolae Carpathia welcomed dignitaries from around the world and congratulated the Israelis.

"Look," Bruce said, pointing to Eli and Moishe. The two witnesses slowly walked to the temple side of the Golden Gate, much to the disdain of the crowd. They were jeered and hissed and booed, but no one dared approach, let alone try to harm them.

"This should be interesting," Bruce said. "I don't think those two have been away from the Wailing Wall more than once."

The crowd murmured as the witnesses

approached. Judd thought Nicolae Carpathia sensed something.

"Israel has rebuilt the temple to hasten the return of their Messiah," Eli and Moishe suddenly shouted in unison, "not realizing that the true Messiah has already come!"

The crowd near the witnesses shrank back, while others continued their shouting against them.

"Israel has built a temple of rejection!" Eli and Moishe continued. "Israel remains largely unbelieving and will soon suffer for it!"

Carpathia's eyes flashed as he railed, "Do not let these vagabonds of violence detract from this momentous day, my friends!"

Without microphones, Eli and Moishe spoke loudly enough for all to hear, crying out in the courtyard as they drowned out Carpathia with their words.

"Enemy of God," they called, "you yourself will one day defile and desecrate this temple!"

"Nonsense!" Nicolae said. He turned to those behind him, clearly frustrated. "Is there not a military leader in Israel with the forti-tude to silence these two?"

Judd strained to hear as the Israeli prime minister stepped forward. "Sir, we have become a weaponless society."

"These two are weaponless as well!"
Nicolae thundered. "Subdue them!"

But Eli and Moishe continued, "God does
not dwell in temples made with hands!"

Bruce turned to Judd. "We needed to be
here. The news media won't show all of this.
Our Web site may be the only place people
can get the true picture of what's happened."

"Do you wish to listen to me or to them?"
Nicolae yelled to the crowd.

"You, Potentate! You!"

"There is no potentate but God himself!"
Eli responded.

And Moishe added, "Your blood sacrifices
shall turn to water, and your water-drawing
to blood!"

Before leaving Israel, Judd returned to the
home of Rabbi Tsion Ben-Judah to interview
the rabbi's stepchildren for the *Underground*.

Dan and Nina seemed overjoyed to see
Judd again, but he could tell they were
nervous about something.

"We live under suspicion," Nina said. "And
it has become worse. Our neighbors have
stopped helping us go to and from the
house."

"The threats against my father are growing," Dan said. "We have talked about the possibility of coming to your country."

Judd gave them his phone number and E-mail address. "If you need to leave, get in touch," he said. "My friends and I would love to help."

THREE

Ryan's Place

THE secret place. Ryan Daley felt most at home there now. The only drawback was that he couldn't take Phoenix with him. Phoenix's bark would give them away. In the middle of stacks of Bibles, Ryan could disappear for hours. *Not that anyone would care*, he thought. *They're all so busy, they don't think about me.*

This was his place to think. To read. He kept pictures of his parents hidden away and remembered life before the world changed. He had lived through an incredible thirteenth year. His mom and dad were dead. His best friend had been raptured. And Lionel, who was both friend and foe at times, had left Global Community Middle School for Nicolae High, so Ryan felt alone. Judd was either traveling with Bruce or buried in his studies. Vicki had been gone a long time and now lived in a different house.

Ryan was changing as well. He had grown taller and leaner over the summer, only a few inches shorter than Judd. The rest of the Young Trib Force didn't call him "little guy" anymore. His voice embarrassed him. He tried to keep it low, but at the worst times it cracked and made him want to keep quiet.

Ryan counted most on Bruce Barnes and Chloe Steele. Bruce spent his time studying, preparing for sermons, or traveling. But Chloe had occasionally taken time for Ryan while Vicki had been gone. Chloe was the older sister of his best friend, Raymie.

"Do you ever think of them?" Ryan asked one day. "Your mom and your little brother?"

"All the time," Chloe had said. "When I see you, it makes me wonder what Raymie would look like now."

"Bet it's hard to be around me," he said.

"Just the opposite," Chloe said.

Now Ryan sat alone, surrounded by Bibles he had confiscated from abandoned homes. He had been studying the book of Acts with Bruce and was fascinated with the miraculous things God had done in the lives of the early Christians. He wanted God to do the same with him.

He read in Acts 2: "'And it shall come to pass in the last days, says God, that I will pour out of My spirit on all flesh. Your sons and your daughters shall prophesy, your young men shall see visions, your old men shall dream dreams.'"

Ryan asked Bruce later that day, "Does that mean I'm going to have a vision?"

"Not necessarily," Bruce said. "But God has already shown himself in a miraculous way in your life."

"How?" Ryan said.

"In Joel it says that God will give signs in the earth—blood and fire and clouds of smoke. The sun will darken, and the moon will become bloodred before Jesus returns."

"I'd like to see that," Ryan said.

"It'll be a terrible day," Bruce said. "But look at Acts 2:21: 'And it shall come to pass that whoever calls on the name of the Lord shall be saved.' That's what happened to you. I'd say that's a miracle."

Vicki met with Chloe Steele soon after she returned. Chloe had worked side by side with Bruce and wanted to bring Vicki up to speed on the changes within the adult Tribulation Force.

"I'm worried about my dad," Chloe said. "He lives here but flies *Global Community One* out of New York. It's hard on him. Plus, working for Carpathia is difficult."

"Why does he do it?"

"He believes that's what God wants."

"What about your relationship with Mr. Williams?" Vicki said.

Chloe shook her head. "My dad says he may be married before Buck and I are."

"Your dad? Marry who?"

"Amanda White," Chloe said. "She knew my mom. It took my dad some time, but they're getting serious."

"Buck hasn't proposed?" Vicki said.

"No, and I'm not going to push him. The night he left for New York he told me he wished I could come with him."

"Why didn't you?"

"*That* would have been appropriate," Chloe said, sarcastically. "Anyway, being apart has helped me love him even more."

"At least you know how he feels, right?"

Chloe blushed.

"What?" Vicki said. "Tell me."

"I was helping him pack. We'd held hands but never kissed. I told him he wouldn't miss me as much as I would miss him, and he dropped his packing tape and looked at me. He said there was no possible way I could care for him more than he cared for me. And then he said, 'You are my whole life. I love you, Chloe.'"

"Ohhhh," Vicki said as she scooted in her chair and rubbed her arms. "Do you think you'll get married?"

"We know the time is short," Chloe said. "If God thinks we can work better together than apart, I want it too. But I'm not going to chase him. There's too much to do to waste time looking out for myself."

Judd was impressed with how Lionel and Ryan had taken over the Web site. During studies with Bruce, the two furiously took notes. Soon Bruce's teachings were on the Web site.

They worked hard at using graphics and animation as well. Lionel and Ryan scrolled Bruce's Scripture references at the bottom of the screen. And they added icons linking news stories to the prophecies.

The Web site seemed risk-free because John and Mark had set up a system so they couldn't be traced. Lionel and Ryan answered E-mails and sent information to those who asked. Many of the hits came from readers of the *Underground* at Nicolae High. Word had also spread to surrounding schools, and the kids saw messages from other states and even other countries.

But the *Underground* became more risky. Because of their dwindling money, the Young Tribulation Force scaled back their distribution to only once a month. And they had to be more and more creative getting it to students. One month they printed business cards with the Web site address and placed them on car windshields and in the seats of school buses. Another month they placed copies of the *Underground* inside popular magazines and books in the library. No one knew where the *Underground* would show up next.

Judd worried about the reaction to Bruce's warnings. Judd expected the Global Community to call Bruce a "kook" and even "hateful," but it seemed even many believers were tired of his gloom and doom predictions.

"I don't care what others think," Bruce said at their next meeting. "We have another year of peace before the next three horsemen of the Apocalypse appear. Once that happens, seventeen more judgments will come."

Judd handed Bruce an E-mail from the Web site. "What do we say to this guy?"

Bruce studied the paper and frowned.

"Everybody has his or her own interpretation of the Bible," the message read. "Stop trying to scare people into believing what you believe."

"Don't respond," Bruce said. "People didn't believe Jesus was who he said he was before the Rapture. Why should it be different now?"

"Because of all that's happened," Vicki said. "I can't believe people can't see."

Bruce asked Judd to insert a video of coverage from the temple in Israel. "Remember what Eli and Moishe predicted would happen when Nicolae dedicated the temple?" Bruce said.

"Something about blood turning to water and water turning to blood, right?"

Bruce nodded. "Watch this."

Judd was amazed to see a sacrificed heifer's blood turning to water. In another ceremony, a high priest recoiled as water drawn into a pail turned dark red. The man's movement made the blood splash, and it splashed and stained his robe.

"Wow," Ryan said, "but what does all the blood and water stuff mean?"

"The Jews who don't believe Jesus is Messiah have gone back to sacrificing animals to show their devotion to God," Bruce said. "What they're doing is rejecting the sacrifice Jesus made on the cross. They're doing it their own way, and that's displeasing to God."

"But why does it have to be blood?" Ryan said.

"Blood is the symbol of forgiveness," Bruce said. "In the Old Testament it says there is no forgiveness of sin without the shedding of blood. That's why Jesus had to die. By turning the blood to water—something powerless—God is showing his disapproval of the sacrifices in the new temple."

"The Israelis are blaming the witnesses for it," Judd said.

"But it's their unbelief and rejection of Jesus as Savior that are to blame," Bruce said. "Nicolae Carpathia has urged Buck Williams to use *Global Community Weekly* to speak out against the intrusion of Moishe and Eli."

Ryan approached Bruce after the meeting. "We're gonna be together now, right?" he said. "You and Vicki and Judd and everybody from now on."

Bruce put a hand on Ryan's shoulder. "I'd like to think we'll all see the glorious appearing of Jesus at the end of the Tribulation," he said, "but I can't promise. Many will die for their beliefs before Christ returns. It's already happening."

Ryan nodded and ran to the car. "Why does Lionel always get to sit up front?" he said.

"Lionel was here first," Judd said. "Don't start."

Later in Ryan's room, Lionel said, "What's bothering you?"

"Nothin'," Ryan said, staring at the computer screen.

Lionel sat on Ryan's bed. "Lonely without me at school?

Ryan nodded. "All the excitement's at Nicolae High."

"It's more boring than you think," Lionel said. "Judd says you're doing a good job on the Web site."

"He never told me that," Ryan said as he clicked the mouse. The images of two men appeared before a cyber Wailing Wall. Eli and Moishe quoted Scripture and proclaimed Jesus as the Messiah.

"Pretty impressive," Lionel said.

"I can do more than that," Ryan said. "Right now all I'm good for is answering E-mails and handing out used Bibles."

"Where is your stash, anyway?" Lionel said. "Am I going to have to follow you someday?"

Ryan smiled. "No way," he said. "Only one person has a clue, and I'm not telling."

FOUR

Surprise Guest

VICKI was closely watched from the day she set foot again in Nicolae High. Judd insisted she not be part of writing or distributing the *Underground*, so when she found a copy in her gym locker, she was as surprised as anyone.

But Vicki did not stop talking about God in class or in private. Some students began to seek her out and ask questions. Others called her names. When one girl discovered she had been adopted by Bruce Barnes, Vicki became known as "Preacher's girl." Vicki only smiled.

The shock of the new year was Mrs. Waltonen. At first, Vicki wanted nothing to do with the woman, but over time, Vicki felt sorry for her. When Vicki saw her, she spoke kindly. They didn't talk one-on-one like before, but Vicki sensed a change and hoped they would.

In late November Bruce sat Vicki and Chaya down in his office. "I have a surprise for you," Bruce said. "I've been in contact with Janie."

"How is she?" Vicki said.

"You'll find out for yourself tomorrow," Bruce said. "She's coming here to live."

Bruce told them he had negotiated with the juvenile facility. He went before a judge and agreed to take full responsibility for Janie's actions while she was in his care. The system was so full of troubled kids, his offer was readily accepted by the authorities.

"But we need to set some rules," he said. "Chaya, this is where you come in."

When Janie arrived the next day, Vicki was excited. Janie seemed cautious as she walked into Bruce's house. "Nice place," she said.

Bruce laid out the rules. There would be no tobacco, no drugs, no alcohol.

Janie shrugged. "No problem."

But Janie bucked the rules. That night Vicki found her on the front step, smoking.

"Bruce said no smoking in the house," Janie said. "I'm not *in* the house."

At school, Janie quickly made friends with the druggie crowd, wore sloppy clothes, and used vulgar language.

Chaya wouldn't let Janie get away with bringing booze or drugs into the house. But Chaya couldn't be with her all day.

Janie seemed bored with the Bible and spiritual things. She sat through Bible studies and church, sighing or even sleeping. Vicki began wondering how long Bruce would let Janie stay.

"I feel responsible for her," Vicki told Bruce after a Young Trib Force meeting. "I thought she'd change."

"God loved us before we ever loved him," Bruce said. "Let's keep showing Janie a little of God's love."

Meanwhile, Vicki felt new emotions about Judd. He was something special. She had always thought so. But he'd graduate the following June, and he wasn't the kind of guy to stay home and vegetate.

Chaya had helped Vicki sort through her feelings. She tried to adopt the same attitude as Chloe Steele had toward Buck. If something happened between Vicki and Judd, fine. If God wanted something totally different for her, she would follow God. But she couldn't help sneaking a prayer in every now and then.

"Lord, if it's OK with you, I pray Judd and I would become more than just friends."

Judd invited everyone to Thanksgiving dinner, but Vicki quickly shot down that idea.

"Ever cooked a bird?" Vicki asked.

"There's a first time for everything," Judd said.

"Just bring dessert to Bruce's place," Vicki said. "I'll get Shelly to help me."

The table looked fabulous on Thanksgiving Day, which the Global Community and Nicolae High now called Fall Festival Day.

"I don't remember anything like this since my family left," Lionel said.

"Where's Janie?" Bruce asked as they stood behind their chairs.

"Still sleeping," Vicki said.

They held hands as Bruce prayed.

"Father, our country and our world no longer celebrate this day, but we do. . . ."

During the meal, talk turned to Nicolae High. They scoffed at the upcoming "winter holiday" and how far the school went to make sure the word *Christmas* was never mentioned.

"We gonna do a Christmas edition of the *Underground?*" Ryan said.

Judd nodded, smiling. "But don't tell Vicki," he whispered.

Shelly said, "No matter how much the Global Community wants people to forget, they still remember it's Christmas. What if we printed an edition that goes outside the school? I work in the office, and there's a master list of addresses for every student, parent, faculty member, and employee. We could mail it."

"Good idea," Judd said, "but the postage cost alone could sink us."

Bruce shrugged. "If God wants you to do it, he can make it happen."

"What about Shelly?" John said. "When the faculty finds out they all got the same mailing, they could trace the list to her."

"Everybody's in the phone book," Shelly said. "I'll take the risk."

Everyone turned as Janie scuffed into the room in her pajamas. She rubbed at her eyes and yawned. "Why didn't somebody tell me it was time for breakfast?"

※

After the Sunday morning service, Bruce pulled Judd aside. "I brought up your idea with a few church leaders," he said, "and someone's given an anonymous gift to cover the postage."

That afternoon Judd and the others went

to work. They concentrated on the prophecies about Jesus' birth. In simple language
they laid out the same claim Dr. Tsion
Ben-Judah had made. Jesus, the son of
Joseph and Mary, was God in the flesh. Not
only had he come to earth and died for
people's sins, but he was coming again.

The mailing went out the week before
Christmas. By the twenty-fourth there were
hundreds more hits on the Web page.

Ryan found Judd in the living room late on
Christmas Eve. A fire crackled in the fire-
place. Judd had pulled out an artificial tree
from the attic, and it stood in the corner with
no ornaments.

"What's up?" Ryan said, carrying a nicely
wrapped box.

"Just thinking," Judd said.

"Whose name did you get for the gift
exchange?" Ryan said.

"It's a secret," Judd said, ignoring the box.
"Think you have enough Bibles for everybody who responded to the mailing?"

"Sure. People are supposed to come by
the church office. Took a bunch there yesterday."

Judd stared at the tree. "Christmas used to

be so important to me," he said. "I'd make a list of all the stuff I wanted. The only surprise was what color my parents wrapped the boxes."

"Man, you were lucky."

Judd closed his eyes. "My dad had the money to buy whatever I wanted," he said. "Now all I remember is my Mom playing Christmas songs on the piano. My dad on the floor playing with Marc and Marcie. Christmas Eve service. Passing out candles and lighting them, one person to the next."

"My dad never played any games with me," Ryan said. "He always brought stuff home from the office to work on. Mom worked, too. They tried to make it up to me at Christmas, so I got some pretty neat stuff. The closest I ever got to church was going over to Raymie's house."

"If I ever have kids—," Judd said.

"What?" Ryan said.

"Ah, it doesn't matter. Neither of us has to worry about being a father, good or bad."

Ryan flicked on the television and saw the leader of the new Enigma Babylon One World Faith, Pontifex Maximus Peter, formerly Peter Mathews of Cincinnati, praise the Global Community's religious unity.

"For you watching in North America," the

man said, "I applaud your embracing Enigma
Babylon One World Faith. Many have abandoned the old traditions for a new belief—
love and light for all people of all nations.
For those who still hold to the old ways,
I urge you to come to the light. Let us put
away the division."

Pontifex Maximus introduced a video clip
from a pastor in Maryland.

"I'm the leader of a congregation that
used to tell people God could only be
known one way," the pastor said. "Thank-
fully, we're now following a new way led by
the example of Potentate Nicolae Carpathia.
And I urge anyone not committed to the
beliefs of the Global Community to accept
them now as we begin a new year and a new
era of peace."

Judd checked E-mail before going to bed. He
found a message from Nina in Israel.

"There have been more threats to my
father's life, but he feels God's protection.
Where would we stay if we decided to come
to your country?"

Judd typed a quick note saying Nina, Dan,
and her parents could stay with someone in
the church. He could help make it happen
anytime they felt it necessary.

✳

Christmas decorations filled Bruce's house.
Late Christmas morning the Young Trib
Force gathered to exchange gifts. Janie com-
plained about not having money to buy any-
thing good and didn't want to participate.
She stayed in her room.

Vicki was chosen to open her gift first. She
eyed the slender box excitedly. It looked like
jewelry, and she hoped Judd had drawn her
name.

Inside she found a gold necklace with one
charm—a cross. "Oh, it's beautiful," Vicki
said, holding it up to her neck and looking at
Judd. "I love it."

Ryan stormed from the room.

"Oh no," Vicki said. "I thought—"

Judd shook his head. "Sorry. I drew someone else's name."

Vicki heard a scream upstairs, and Ryan
came running, then slammed the front door
behind him.

Janie appeared at the top of the stairs.
"That little creep!" she said. "He didn't even
knock."

Vicki ran into the cold and followed Ryan's
tracks in the snow. She found him shivering
at a bus stop at the end of the street.

"She cussed at me," Ryan said. "How was I supposed to know it was her room?"

"You didn't," Vicki said. "I'm sorry about Janie. And I really do like the necklace. How'd you get the money?"

"I didn't take it—honest," Ryan said.

"I didn't think you stole it," Vicki said. "It just looks like it cost a lot."

"Saved it," Ryan said. Vicki could see his breath as Ryan looked straight ahead. "The guy at the store made me promise not to tell he sold me something with a cross on it." He sighed and shook his head. "Janie yelled at me because I caught her. She was smoking something up there."

By the time they got home, Janie had aired out the room and disposed of whatever she had been smoking.

"Ryan's a liar," Janie said. "I didn't do anything."

FIVE

Race for the Top

Four Months Later

JUDD looked at the test questions, and his heart sank. He knew the answers, but the truth wasn't what his teacher, Mr. Syncrete, wanted. Judd had had no problems all year in trigonometry or English. He had a running feud with the biology teachers over evolution, but he could back up his beliefs with scientific data. Religion class threatened his dream of becoming valedictorian.

Judd proudly wore the cross in Mr. Syncrete's class. The Global Community required religious education for graduation. Judd struggled not to make waves, but at times he couldn't keep silent.

The class had begun with an overview of the Enigma Babylon One World Faith. Mr.

Syncrete praised its leader, Pontifex Maximus Peter, for ushering in what he called a "new era of tolerance and unity" among all major religions. Mr. Syncrete spent hours on Eastern religions and spoke in glowing terms of animistic beliefs—that even objects have a soul. Guest lecturers explained everything from worship of ancestors to yoga. But the teacher's demeanor soured when he covered Judaism. And when Christianity finally came up, his attitude got even worse.

"The Jews believe in one God who let them be annihilated in the Holocaust," Mr. Syncrete said with a sneer. "And the Christians have three Gods who did the same. It's an irrational, superstitious belief system."

According to Mr. Syncrete, the biggest enemies of the new one-world faith were the millions who believed Jesus was the only way to God. He scoffed at those who dared disagree. He read word for word the statement of Pontifex Maximus Peter concerning Christians:

To say arbitrarily, Pope Peter wrote, *that the Jewish and Protestant Bible, containing only the Old and New Testaments, is the final authority for faith and practice, represents the height of intolerance and disunity. It flies in the face of all we have accomplished. Those who agree with that false doctrine are hereby considered heretics.*

Spats between Judd and Mr. Syncrete were legendary. No matter what the argument, Judd came back to the Resurrection. Jesus was the only spiritual leader to prove his claims of divinity.

"You have no basis for saying that," Mr. Syncrete said once. "Give me one shred of evidence that the so-called Resurrection isn't the work of fishermen turned fiction writers."

"I'll give you the evidence," Judd said, "if you'll admit that the resurrection of Jesus, if it happened, changes everything you're teaching."

Judd had the man in a corner. If Mr. Syncrete admitted that rising from the dead would prove the claims of Christ, Judd could show that Jesus was a real person who had risen from the dead. If he didn't let Judd speak, Mr. Syncrete would look like a coward.

"We'll come back to this," Mr. Syncrete had said finally. Everyone snickered. They never got back to the question, and from that day on, Judd knew Mr. Syncrete was out to fail him.

While the Young Tribulation Force cheered Judd's efforts, Bruce cautioned him. "You don't win hearts by winning arguments. It's important to know the truth and tell it, but you can't use it to hurt. Speak the truth in love."

Judd answered the multiple-choice questions on his final. On a couple he put asterisks and wrote notes at the bottom of the page: "This is the view taught in class, not my point of view." But the final essay question made his blood boil: "Enigma Babylon One World Faith encompasses all religions and is thus superior to all individual belief systems. Explain why you believe this."

Judd rose and approached the teacher's desk.

"Sit down, Mr. Thompson," Mr. Syncrete said.

"But this is not a fair question. It assumes—"

"I said sit down!"

"It may be your job," Judd said, "but I won't be brainwashed."

"Give me your test."

Judd handed it to him.

"You are excused. The final is half your grade. You've just failed the class."

Judd went straight to Mr. Kurtz, the dean of students. Mr. Kurtz was a Santa-like figure with a big, round belly and a white beard. He could be tough, but Judd respected him. Judd explained as Mr. Kurtz stroked his beard.

"I've been watching the grade point averages, and you're a lock," Mr. Kurtz said. "The only thing that could possibly come between you and the top of your class is an F."

"I don't think it's a fair question," Judd said. "It makes the wrong assumption—that I agree."

Mr. Kurtz shrugged.

"You can go back and apologize, throw yourself on his mercy, and answer the thing, or take your lumps."

"I have no other choice?"

"You could go to the school board, but graduation would be long over by the time they could act on your complaint. Looks like you have to choose."

Judd hurried back to class. He had only five minutes left.

Toward the end of a study period, Vicki heard a commotion and followed her teacher into the hall. A Global Community guard rifled through Janie's locker. Janie stood nearby yelling, "You have no right!"

Before Vicki could get to her, Mrs. Jenness led Janie to the office.

"Back to class," the teacher said.

Vicki turned and nearly ran into Judd.

"Sorry," Judd said. "I don't have time to explain, but pray for me."

Only a handful of students were still taking the test when Judd returned. Mr. Syncrete didn't look up. Only three minutes left in the class.

"Mr. Kurtz suggested I apologize, throw myself on your mercy."

Mr. Syncrete sat back in his chair and put a pencil to his lips. He smiled. "You have been a burr in my saddle from day one. And now you have the audacity to ask for mercy?"

"I'm sorry, sir. I was wrong. I'm passionate about this, and I want people to consider what I believe. But I didn't do it the right way. Forgive me."

Mr. Syncrete looked at the clock. "It would not be fair to allow you extra time. After all, you walked out."

"Then just count the multiple choice," Judd said.

The bell rang. Others filed past and added their tests to the stack. Mr. Syncrete scratched his head, pursed his lips, and nodded.

Vicki waited for Janie outside the principal's office after school. Mrs. Waltonen nodded as she passed, then returned a few minutes later.

"She should be out in a couple of minutes," Mrs. Waltonen said.

"Thanks. They've been in there a long time."

"They found something in her locker. You probably should prepare for the worst."

Vicki hung her head. Months of trying to be Janie's friend, talking, pleading, and accepting her hadn't changed her a bit. Vicki was surprised to see Mrs. Waltonen still standing there.

"I want to say," the woman began haltingly, "that—well, I appreciate what you've tried to do for that girl."

Before Vicki could thank her, Mrs. Waltonen slipped away as Judd approached.

"Finish your last final?" Vicki said.

Judd nodded. Mr. Kurtz stepped out and waved Judd inside.

"He doesn't look happy," Vicki said.

"This is it," Judd said.

A few moments later Bruce came into the office. Vicki felt strange to greet him there. She told him what had happened in the hall.

"This has been brewing for some time," Bruce said. "We've disciplined her and done everything humanly possible. Now there have to be consequences."

"I'll wait for you," she said.

"Why would my daughter wait out here?" he said, motioning her in with him.

Mrs. Jenness told them in front of Janie that the girl had hidden drugs in her locker. Janie would be sent back to the care of the Northside Detention Center.

"They'll send me downstate," Janie said. "Please, I won't do it again."

"Can we have a moment?" Bruce said.

Mrs. Jenness stepped out. Bruce looked straight at Janie. "I've tried to help you. I've given you a home. Vicki and Chaya love you more than I could ever have imagined."

"I'll change," Janie said. "I mean it this time."

"I hope you will, Janie," Bruce said. "I pray every day that you will turn to Christ. We've done all we can for you. It's hard to let you go, knowing how you'll be treated—"

Bruce's lip quivered. "The truth will set you free. But you have to accept the truth for yourself."

Janie sobbed as she was taken away. Bruce and Vicki watched the van drive away.

Judd met them outside.

"One of the hardest things you'll ever have to do," Bruce said, "is to let go of someone you care deeply about."

Vicki asked Judd what Mr. Kurtz said.

"Good news and bad news," Judd said. "I

didn't make valedictorian; I came in second.
But I get to speak at graduation as salutatorian."

SIX

Podium Drama

JUDD's first draft of his speech was thirteen pages long. Single-spaced. He would have to cut more than half of it. He had only seven minutes to speak.

The valedictorian, Marjorie Amherst, wasn't a believer. Her parents sponsored a Global Community organization. Mark called them "Nicolae nuts." They had written and called Global Community headquarters for months. The rumor on campus was that Leon Fortunato, aide to Nicolae Carpathia himself, might actually attend the ceremony.

Judd was so engrossed in his speech that he had little time to think about his money problems. Everyone had pitched in, but two or three more mortgage payments, and they were sunk.

Lionel and Ryan popped in with suggestions for his speech.

"I can't wait to see you up there givin' it to 'em!" Ryan said.

"Sorry, pal," Judd said. "I get only two tickets, and I've already asked Bruce and Vicki."

"Every time—," Ryan said.

"Can't we just stand in the back?" Lionel said.

"It's nothing personal," Judd said. "Maybe you can see it on TV, especially if this Fortunato guy shows up."

Judd cut his speech to five pages. Still too long. Mrs. Jenness looked at the content, too. The next day Judd was called into her office.

"Limit your remarks to the school and what you've learned here," Mrs. Jenness said. "Cut the religious content."

"What do you consider 'religious'?"

"Mentions of God. About the disappearances being a 'wake-up call.' Don't offend any special guests."

* * *

Vicki asked to meet with Mrs. Waltonen during gym class. Mrs. Waltonen let the student teacher take over and showed Vicki to her office.

"About what happened," Vicki said. "I want you to know I don't hold anything against you."

"We came down hard on you," Mrs. Waltonen said. "I thought you deserved it at the time. You've healed from your wounds?"

"The stitches came out, but the detention center stays with me. At night I wake up sometimes. And I think about Janie a lot."

"Any word from her?"

"They took her downstate. I've written, but she hasn't written back."

Mrs. Waltonen lifted a snapshot from her desk.

"My granddaughter," she said. "Gone."

"I'm sorry."

"I've been thinking a lot about what you said to me last year. Coach Handlesman told me the same thing. My family members are in heaven. I wasn't ready to hear it."

"I would have thought it would make you feel better."

"I was angry. I'm not sure with whom. I looked at Christians as the enemy. You were telling me something I couldn't stand, something I didn't want to hear."

Vicki wanted to quote Mrs. Waltonen a million verses, but she held back. "How about now?" Vicki said.

"Well," Mrs. Waltonen said, "I've slipped into your church a few times."

"You're kidding!" Vicki said.

"I saw the tape your former pastor made. I've got it all down."

"So now what?"

"I want to believe like you so I can see my family again. But it's all too fantastic, too hard to believe."

"Harder than to believe your family was taken right out of their clothes?"

Mrs. Waltonen leaned back, and her chair squeaked.

＊

Security was tight at the graduation ceremony. From behind the curtain, Judd watched Global Community guards herd everyone through metal detectors. Some parents forgot their tickets and still expected to get in. They were turned away, furious.

Someone tapped on Judd's shoulder. He was surprised to see Coach Handlesman.

"Hey," Judd said, "what are you doing here?"

"I'm out on good behavior," he said, chuckling. "I couldn't miss such an important night for you. I'm really proud. Can't wait to hear what you're going to say."

Judd shook his head. "Mrs. Jenness hacked everything important out of my speech. I wanted to really say something."

"You'll sure have an audience," Mr. Handlesman said. "Those are network news cameras. I hear that CNN is airing the Global Community guy live."

"I'm on just before him," Judd said. "I might just say what I want."

"Whatever you do," Mr. Handlesman said, "know that we're behind you."

Mrs. Jenness came through the curtains and clapped. The honored graduates came to attention.

Mr. Handlesman was gone.

Vicki and Bruce sat near the front. Camera crews partially blocked their view. Mary Lee Manwether, brown hair perfectly in place, jotted notes and spoke with her producer.

"If they stick with the time on the program," the producer said, "you'll have about a minute to fill before Fortunato speaks."

Mary Lee didn't look up.

As the strains of "Pomp and Circumstance" filled the room, Judd and Marjorie followed Mrs. Jenness and the faculty advisors onstage.

"Who put up the new curtain over the stage?" Mrs. Jenness whispered. "Very nice."

Leon Fortunato, dressed in a sleek, dark

suit, slipped in at the last moment with an entourage of bodyguards. The audience tittered, then broke into wild applause as he was led to a chair on the stage. He bowed slightly to the crowd, then was seated.

"I can't believe I'm in the same room with him," Marjorie Amherst gushed. "He actually works side by side with Nicolae Carpathia! Am I pale, Judd? I might just keel over."

"Down, girl," Judd said. "He's just a man."

"If I get too nervous, can you take my place?" she whispered. "I don't know if I can do this."

"You'll be fine," Judd said.

"I'm serious, Judd. I think I'm going to be ill."

"How about I let you go first," Judd said. "If you have a problem, I'll come up and help."

Marjorie squeezed his hand with a look that oozed her thanks.

Judd scratched the plan to Mrs. Jenness on the back of his program and passed it to her. Mrs. Jenness frowned and looked at Judd. He stuck his finger in his mouth and pointed at Marjorie. Marjorie weaved in her seat and looked like a ghost. Mrs. Jenness pursed her lips and nodded.

Vicki gave a little wave, but Judd didn't acknowledge her. He looked toward someone in the graduating class, nodded, then sat back. Vicki looked at the row of seniors in front of her and noticed John a few seats away. He had in his hand some kind of a control device with an antenna.

"What's going on?" Vicki mouthed when she caught his eye.

John put a finger to his lips.

Judd tried to calm Marjorie as two students sang an original song about their years at Nicolae Carpathia High School. Mrs. Jenness beamed as one strummed a guitar and the other sang:

> Nicolae, you and I have shared so much together.
> We will sing, we will work to make this world much better.
> Till the day that I die, I will not forget Nicolae. Nicolae. Nicolae.

Mr. and Mrs. Amherst applauded before the song was over. They stood, but no one else did until Leon Fortunato also rose. Mrs. Jenness alerted the audience to a change in the program and introduced the valedictorian.

Marjorie was shaky. She made it to the

lectern, turned to curtsey to Leon Fortunato, and fell in a heap at his feet. Her mother and father rushed to the stage, but Global Community guards blocked them. Marjorie was taken backstage. Mrs. Jenness, flustered, introduced Leon Fortunato next instead of Judd. The man looked at his program, then stood and thanked the audience for a standing ovation.

Vicki saw the frantic look on the reporter's face.

"Give it to us now, he's up," Mary Lee Manwether told her producer.

"They just went live to another report from New Babylon," the producer shot back. "What happened?"

"The program's out the window because the girl flopped," Mary Lee said. "Can't somebody get this guy to wait?"

"The tape's rolling," the producer said. "We'll be OK."

Someone shushed the two as Leon Fortunato began. Vicki thought he looked more like a character actor than a politician. He was thick and swarthy with his hair slicked back, and he had the air of someone used to being the center of attention. He had an accent, but Vicki couldn't place it.

"I bring you greetings from New Babylon

and the man this school was named for, Global Community Potentate Nicolae Carpathia."

The audience applauded.

"Graduates, your parents and teachers have invested countless hours in your education. Today, we salute you all."

"Slick," Vicki said.

"Too slick," Bruce whispered.

Fortunato looked at the graduates. "I speak for Potentate Carpathia and the entire Global Community when I extend an invitation for you to help us answer the question that has plagued this world since time began.

"In this extraordinary moment in world history, we have within our grasp the opportunity to, as your singers suggested, 'make this world much better.'"

Mrs. Jenness got Judd's attention. She shrugged and said, "Be ready. You're next."

Judd nodded and glanced toward John in the audience. Judd lowered his head and coughed into his gown. John nodded slightly.

Judd knew he would never have this opportunity again.

"And so I thank the faculty and staff of Nicolae Carpathia High School," Leon

Fortunato said, "for staying true to the cause Potentate Carpathia and I strive for daily. May your efforts bear fruit for the sake of peace, for the sake of this country, and for the sake of our world."

As the audience stood in wild applause, Vicki saw a red light on the camera. Mary Lee Manwether said, "We're ready with a videotape of a speech from Nicolae Carpathia's right-hand man—"As Mrs. Jenness rose to introduce Judd, the producer gave Mary Lee the "stretch" sign. Something was wrong.

"All right," Mary Lee said. "We'll get to that in just a moment. Meanwhile, let's listen to one of the students of Nicolae Carpathia High, uh . . . this is Marjorie . . . no . . . I'm sorry, this is Judd Thompson, the salutatorian."

Judd took a deep breath. Leon Fortunato politely applauded and looked at his watch. Judd caught a glimpse of Vicki and Bruce, spied Coach Handlesman toward the back, and glanced at teachers who had lived through the most tumultuous year on the planet.

It was decision time. Judd saw the CNN camera trained on him. He could do only what he believed was right.

SEVEN

The Speech

JOHN and Mark had studied the sound system in the auditorium. If Judd deviated from his script, Mrs. Jenness would intervene. They had to have an alternate plan.

Mark and John had rigged an auxiliary microphone, hidden under Judd's graduation gown. If his podium microphone was turned off, the auxiliary bypassed the mixing board and went straight to the huge overhead monitors. Then, the only way to keep Judd from being heard would be to cut the speaker cable.

A thousand images flashed through Judd's mind as he stepped to the lectern. Empty seats on the plane. Losing his parents. Bruce. Pastor Billings's tape. Vicki and Lionel and Ryan.

The crowd stared, and the red light on the

television camera beckoned. Whatever the cost, whatever the outcome, he felt God had called him to this moment.

Judd remembered a few techniques from speech class. He let the audience settle, then paused another second. The auditorium stilled as he folded his notes and placed them inside the lectern. He would speak from memory and from his heart.

"I made a promise to myself in this room one year ago. I vowed to deliver a message tonight. And I thank G—I'm thankful I'm able to do that."

No looking down. Judd looked at their faces.

"When we graduates started our junior year, we had no idea that many of our friends would not join us tonight. Kids we went to grade school with. Kids we played T-ball with. We felt as close to some of them as to our own families. But now they're gone.

"I would like to remember them now with a moment of silence."

Judd stepped back and bowed his head. He turned slightly to see Mrs. Jenness and Leon Fortunato looking at the floor. So far, so good.

"We remember those who are not with us," Judd finally said softly. Then his voice rose. "And now we embark on a new road. As Mr. Fortunato said, we have an opportunity to promote peace. To make this world much better."

Judd grabbed the lectern and with the fervency of an old-time preacher belted out, "We have an opportunity to follow the mandate of the Global Community and its leader, Nicolae Carpathia."

Vicki, stunned, looked at Bruce. Applause filled the auditorium. She saw Leon Fortunato lean down and say something to Mrs. Jenness. Mary Lee Manwether pointed to herself, but her producer rolled a finger in the air and said, "Let it go. This is good."

Bruce said, "Carpathia has certain powers of control. Maybe his right-hand man has learned from him."

Vicki glanced at John. He was smiling.

Judd's heart pounded. He took another breath to calm himself. He made the students laugh with memories of familiar sights and sounds on campus. He poked fun at the keyboard teacher and gave statistics on how many frogs they had dissected in biology class. The faculty laughed along.

"They say confession is good for the soul," Judd said, "and if it's good for the soul, it ought to be good for the Global Community."

Judd looked around and saw Leon Fortunato chuckle. Mrs. Jenness quickly leafed through Judd's script.

"Last year after some of our friends left us behind, someone published and distributed an underground newspaper. It contained some rather outlandish statements."

Mrs. Jenness frantically scanned pages and threw them aside. She stood.

It's too early to be shut down, Judd thought.

Judd continued, "For those who don't know, our administration cracked down on these would-be journalists, and I think it's appropriate to give a round of applause for our principal, Mrs. Jenness."

Mrs. Jenness was caught off guard. She glared at Judd. Then, realizing the camera was on her, she smiled and waved. Reluctantly, she sat.

Vicki held her breath. Was Judd going to give up his friends?

"This is really cool," Ryan said as he and Lionel listened to the applause. "Wish we could be there."

"No way we'd have gotten in," Lionel said. "The place is packed."

"This isn't what he wrote," Ryan said. "This is the speech he didn't show them."

"And how do you know that?" Lionel said, suddenly interested.

"Found it," Ryan said. "It's goin' on the Web as soon as he's finished."

"I carry a secret tonight," Judd continued. "I know the identity of the one who printed, wrote, and helped distribute that paper. One of our teachers last year took the fall for the real culprit, and I feel bad about that. The truth is, the culprit was . . . *me.*"

Vicki heard someone say, "I don't believe it."

"I knew it all the time," another said.

"What's he doing?" Vicki said as Judd called for quiet. The camera was still on. The CNN producer told Mary Lee to sit down.

Bruce said, "It looks like Mrs. Jenness is ready to pull the plug."

Judd glanced back as Mrs. Jenness turned to Leon Fortunato and Leon assured her with a wave.

Judd continued. "A year ago I knew the truth and didn't want to accept it. I have come to believe that the truth will set you free."

Judd told about his plan to run away and about the plane ride to Europe on which scores of passengers disappeared around him.

"We've learned a lot at Nicolae High. We owe a debt to our teachers and parents. But if we gain a whole world of knowledge and miss the most important thing in life, what good will our education be? What if we gain the world but lose our souls?"

"You will make many decisions in the future. But tonight I tell you that there is ultimate truth. If you believe it and act on it, your life will change forever. If you dismiss it, the road ahead is grim."

Judd heard Fortunato say, "OK, that's enough," and Mrs. Jenness approached. He kept going.

"There is one way, one truth, one path to life and peace, and that is through Jesus Christ."

Mrs. Jenness said, "Stop." She drew a finger across her throat at the control board, and AV techies turned knobs, flipped switches, pulled cords, and shrugged.

"I beg you to consider him! He died that you might live."

"Judd, step away from the microphone," Mrs. Jenness said.

Judd stayed where he was. He pointed behind him, and instantly the curtain fell, revealing a banner with the text of a Bible verse, John 3:16.

"For God so loved the world that He gave His only begotten Son, that whoever believes in Him should not perish but have ever-lasting life."

"Someone turn the microphone off!" Mrs. Jenness yelled. Global Community guards approached. Though the microphone was dead, Judd could still be heard.

He heard a scattering of boos and hisses. Judd moved to his right at the edge of the stage and looked into the faces of the gradu-ating class.

"You've read the *Underground*," he said, his voice even louder now through the hidden microphone. "You know that what the Bible predicted is coming true."

Mrs. Jenness screamed through the dead microphone, "Turn him off!"

But Judd's voice rang clear through the hall. "I'm not a rebel," he said. "I'm a truth teller."

Global Community guards rushed the stage. Judd moved left and was blocked from the stairs. He ran right as Fortunato rose and avoided Leon like a running back slipping a tackler.

"God will hear you if you ask him to forgive you," Judd shouted as he ran, breath-ing heavily now. Students hooted and cheered as he eluded the guards. The CNN camera followed him. He slipped into the plants at the edge of the stage. Before him was the drop to the auditorium floor. Guards were upon him.

"If you believe in your heart that Jesus was raised from the dead and confess with your mouth that he is Lord, you will be saved. Don't wait. Pray now!"

Judd heard the footsteps. Mrs. Jenness still shouted. He glanced to see an angry Leon Fortunato escorted by a cadre of bodyguards. A GC guard reached for Judd but got only the edge of his robe. Judd pulled away, heard a rip, and lost his balance. He flipped in the air and landed hard on his feet as he fell to the floor. Pain shot through his right foot.

Vicki jumped out of her seat, but Bruce grabbed her arm.

"Let me go!" she said.

The audience fell silent now. Students craned their necks to see Judd lying under the John 3:16 banner.

"Uh, just another indication of the religious diversity in the country," Mary Lee Manwether said. "And now, I think we have the tape of the remarks made tonight by the Global Community's Leon Fortunato."

As the guards converged upon him, Judd forced himself to speak through the pain.

"Give your life to Christ right now," he gasped. "Pray with me. God, I know I have sinned. . . . I need your forgiveness. Come . . . into my life now . . . change me . . . I accept you now."

As the guards yanked him to his feet, he forced himself into one last act of commitment. One last show of resolve. Judd rolled on his side and put his weight on his good leg. Slowly, painfully, he stood.

"Thank you," he said as the Global Community guards grabbed him and led him away.

Vicki could not hold back her tears. Bruce put an arm around her.

The room was silent except for Judd's heavy breathing into the microphone. The guards were not gentle. One called him a name. Another cursed and told the others to keep quiet.

Then, through her tears, Vicki saw something wonderful. On the other side of the auditorium stood a lone figure—a faculty member.

"Who is that?" Bruce said.

"Mrs. Waltonen," Vicki said.

In the back Coach Handlesman stood and clapped. Bruce and Vicki stood. Then John and Mark in their graduation robes. Throughout the auditorium students and parents stood, some clapping, some weeping. Some sat in silence. Others booed.

Vicki shook. A guard roughly ushered Mrs. Waltonen from the room.

EIGHT

The Militia

JUDD was expelled, given no credit, and barred from any college or university. A Global Community officer looked at him with contempt.

"I hope you're happy," the man said. "You'll never be anything now!"

After hours of detainment, Judd had signed a statement agreeing to cease making public statements of disloyalty to the Global Community. Otherwise he would be sent to prison.

"Do you mean to keep that promise?" Bruce asked as he drove Judd home early the next morning.

"I can keep that promise and still talk about my faith," Judd said. "But if it comes to that, there are worse things than a re-education camp."

"I hope Coach Handlesman and Mrs. Waltonen agree," Bruce said. GC peacekeepers concluded that Mr. Handlesman was to blame for the device that allowed Judd to override the sound system.

The broadcast had been live, so news of Judd's speech spread. He was a hero to believers and a sad figure to others. Fortunato called the event "an isolated incident," but leaked reports said he was furious with the news producer who had called the shots and had her fired from her post. Judd only hoped Nicolae Carpathia heard about it.

Judd didn't want to go to college anyway, not with only a few years left. Bruce asked him to go with him on more trips abroad.

But John wanted to go to college.

"Seems like a waste to me," Mark said. "We have less than seven years left. We ought to make the most of them."

"And your answer is the militia?" John said.

"You bet. The *Underground* helped us get our message out. Let's take it to another level."

Bruce shook his head.

"Tomorrow night we're simulating an attack," Mark said. "I can't say much, but the militia is big. I think God is going to use it to overthrow Carpathia."

"That doesn't square with Scripture," Judd said.

"What are we supposed to do, roll over and play dead?" Mark said. "Come out and go through an exercise with us, Judd. Your ankle's healed."

"I'm not worried about my ankle. I just don't think this is the answer."

"And I think you're chicken."

Vicki jumped in. "And what do the women in your militia do? Stay home and bake cookies?"

"Come along if you'd like," Mark said. "All of you. Bruce, too."

"Cool," Ryan said. "What time do we leave?"

"Sorry," Mark said. "Too young."

"I'll be there," Judd said.

"Me, too," Vicki said.

※

Vicki put on combat fatigues. She painted her face the same colors and surprised Chaya, who was studying in the den.

"You went a little heavy on the green and black," Chaya joked. "What're you trying to prove?"

"Judd and I hope we can show Mark how silly this all is."

73

The moon was full as they drove north. The air was hot and muggy, but the wind felt good as it rushed through the cab of Mark's truck. The militia had grown in the last year, and Mark explained their network. The Midwest was one of the strongest outposts in the country.

"But Carpathia has gathered all the nuclear weapons," Judd said. "What chance could you possibly have? It's like a slingshot against a bazooka."

"You think Global Community has all the nukes?" Mark said with a smile. "The GC won't know what hit 'em. Besides, look what God did once with a slingshot."

They parked in a wooded area in Wisconsin and covered the truck with brush.

"Is this necessary?" Judd said.

Mark didn't answer. He led them through a half mile of woods into a clearing, where a few hundred men in fatigues stood talking. Vicki noticed few women. Major Stockton Evers, a well-built man with close-cropped hair, stood on a small hill to address the group.

"Tonight we simulate a battle strike," he said. He suddenly noticed Judd and Vicki and clenched his teeth.

"Who are these two?"

"Friends of mine," Mark said. "I've told you about—"

"*Anyone* who attends has to go through protocol," Major Evers interrupted. "Especially a meeting as sensitive as this one."

Mark said, "This is Judd Thompson, the one who stood up to Leon Fortunato on television."

Major Evers raised his eyebrows.

"And this is Vicki Byrne, our friend."

"And we can trust them?"

"I would trust my life to them, or I wouldn't have brought them."

Several clapped and patted Judd on the back, but Vicki noticed a few scowls.

"Next time, you check with me before you bring anyone, understand?" Major Evers said.

The man led each squad through grueling paces as they moved through the woods.

"No wonder you're in such good shape," Vicki said as she tried to keep up. Some behind her were laughing.

"You're doing good," Mark said. "Watch for branches and holes up ahead. Don't twist that ankle again, Judd."

An hour into the exercise, Vicki heard something strange and recognized the *thwop-thwop-thwop* of helicopter blades.

"You guys really make this thing realistic," Vicki said.

Mark looked concerned. "Stay here."

The rest of the squad looked confused. First one helicopter, then another appeared. Bright lights shone down as Judd and Vicki shielded their eyes.

"Impressive," Judd said.

Mark ran back to them. "This way," he said, and hurtled through the woods.

"Halt! Stay where you are," a voice boomed from the sky. "This is an unlawful assembly. Lie down with your hands over your heads."

People screamed. A few lay down while others ran.

"This is a joke, right?" Judd yelled, as he and Vicki caught up with Mark.

"No joke," Mark said. A burst of machine gunfire cut small trees in half ahead of them. Mark veered left and shouted, "Keep your heads down and follow me!"

Vicki ran, but her legs felt like lead. Nothing she had ever experienced, not even the disappearance of her family, compared with this terror.

Mark led them to the edge of a cliff. Vicki saw only rocks, then darkness below. A third helicopter now pursued, its lights scanning the trees behind them.

"Come on," Mark yelled as he jumped into the ravine.

"Mark, no!" Vicki screamed, then covered her eyes.

Judd grabbed her arm. "You're next."

In the moonlight Vicki saw Mark below, suspended from a rope. She jumped to a ledge and grabbed the rope. Swinging back and forth, she and Mark made their way down. Halfway to the bottom, Mark disappeared into the face of a rock.

Vicki's heart pounded as first she, then Judd followed Mark into a huge cave just as the helicopter passed.

She tried to catch her breath.

"Mark, come to your senses," Vicki said.

Mark held up his hand. Something was moving behind them. A light shone in their faces.

"You made it," Major Evers said.

"Yes, sir," Mark said. "How about the others?"

"We're checking," Major Evers said. He sat and turned off his light. Vicki heard water trickling and muffled voices deep in the cave.

"The GC means business," Mark said.

"We knew they were onto us," Major Evers said.

"Then why did you take the chance?" Vicki said.

"We let the GC find us. Carpathia will hear there's a couple hundred guys doing push-ups in the woods. He thinks small potatoes. Meanwhile, we plan our assault."

"When?" Judd said.

"I wouldn't tell you if I knew. When the time is right, we'll strike, and with a vengeance."

"Is it true President Fitzhugh is involved with the militia?" Judd said.

Evers squinted at him. "You know I can't divulge that. But our objective is to have him back in the Oval Office within a couple of months." He shook his head. "The way Carpathia has treated that man . . ."

"Why is Carpathia doing this?" Vicki said. "Who do you think he is?"

"I know religious types think he's the Antichrist. Frankly, I don't know, and I don't care. He's taken our country from us. I'd die to get it back."

"If we don't stand up to him," Mark said, "he'll take everything."

A man with a walkie-talkie led Major Evers and the kids to a communications post. Four militia members had been shot. The GC were sending troops on foot and were only a few miles away.

"I'm sorry," Mark said. "If I'd have known, I wouldn't have brought you."

"Try to make it back to your vehicle and get out of here," Major Evers said. "If you get caught, we were just roasting hot dogs."

Mark made the climb up look easy. Judd favored his ankle. Vicki slipped once, but when Judd grabbed her arm, she glared at him and wrenched away.

"I can do it," she said.

As they reached the truck, Mark slid behind the wheel. "Something isn't right," he said. "That was too easy."

He slipped out of the truck and with catlike motion climbed an enormous tree. In a few moments he was back. "It's a trap," he said. "We'll have to find another way out."

"We could hoof it," Vicki said.

"Can't leave the truck," Mark said. "GC would trace it." He pulled a map from the glove compartment. "Head east on foot. After a few miles, you'll come to a stream. Follow that south just across the Illinois border. If I make it through, I'll meet you here, at this overpass."

"Shouldn't we stick together?" Judd said.

"If they catch you," Mark said, "it's off to the reeducation camp. Get going."

Judd heard helicopters in the distance. He and Vicki started off.

"I don't think we convinced him of anything," Vicki whispered.

"Those guys have made up their minds," Judd said.

NINE

Wedding Bells

EVERYONE made it home without incident, but the next day they argued. "What happened last night proves we're doing the right thing," Mark said.

"How can you say that?" Judd said, hardly able to control himself. "It was foolish. All three of us could have been killed! And for what? What did we accomplish?"

"You don't understand," Mark said. "Things are about to change."

"The change has to be spiritual," Judd said. "There are so many constructive things you could do."

"You don't call fighting the Antichrist constructive?" Mark said.

Vicki said, "We're just concerned about you, Mark."

"Think about Lionel and Ryan, too," Judd said. "You're influencing those guys."

✳

Judd slept until afternoon, then headed to the church. He was surprised to find Vicki at the front door. "Keeping watch?" he said.

"You haven't heard about the wedding?" Vicki said.

Vicki explained the romance Judd hadn't seen. He knew Chloe Steele and Buck Williams were seeing each other and even guessed that they might get married. But he hadn't guessed about Amanda White and Rayford Steele. She was a tall, handsome woman about Mr. Steele's age; she had streaked hair and impeccable taste in clothes.

"And it was the most romantic proposal I've ever heard of. Buck surprised Chloe at Amanda's office and proposed to her in one room while her dad was proposing to Amanda in the other. The only problem is, now we're losing Chloe. She and Buck will live in New York."

Judd and Vicki crept to Bruce's office and listened outside the door. Bruce told the couples where to stand and led them through the double ceremony.

"I'm not going to preach a sermon," Bruce

said. "You've heard enough of those. But I do want to challenge you. With what lies ahead, with the uncertainty all around us, cling to each other. Love each other. Forgive each other. Put each other's needs ahead of your own, as Christ did. And let no one, *no one* come between what God has divinely joined."

Judd heard Buck say his vows. Buck's voice was trembling. "Chloe, I promise to love you, and you only. I will honor you above all others, above even my own life. . . . "

Chloe responded with her vows.

Then Rayford pledged himself to Amanda, saying, "I will treasure the gift God has given me in you."

"And I am yours, Rayford," Amanda said, "whether in sickness or in health, for richer or poorer, until death separates us."

Bruce finished by praying, "For this brief flash of joy in a world on the brink of disaster, we thank you and pray your blessing and protection on us all until we meet back here again. Bind our hearts as brothers and sisters in Christ while we are apart."

Judd and Vicki stepped outside the church.

"Makes you wonder, doesn't it?" Judd said.

"Wonder what?" Vicki said.

"You know," Judd said, pawing the ground with his foot. "That kind of stuff."

"What kind of stuff?"

"You know."

"Judd Thompson, this is the first time I've seen you blush."

Vicki let him stammer, then came to his rescue. "You know Captain Steele and Amanda are moving to New Babylon."

"You're kidding," Judd said.

"Carpathia wants all his staff there."

Judd turned to Vicki. "I've always wondered whether—"

But Bruce and the couples came out of the office. "Hey, kids," Bruce said. "I'd like you to meet Rayford and Amanda Steele, and Chloe and Buck Williams."

Vicki looked at Judd and smiled.

❋

Judd and Bruce flew to Australia. In Melbourne thousands of believers crowded the local stadium to hear the American pastor speak. In Sydney the crowds were even greater, but Judd also saw more Global Community peacekeepers.

When they arrived in Jakarta, Indonesia, a team of translators met them and set up their schedule. Judd tried to pick up a few words of each new language they encountered. On the island of Sumatra he tried to say he was Bruce's right-hand man. The locals laughed as the translator informed Judd that he had said, "I am the hand of a chicken."

Judd and Bruce arrived in the middle of dry season. In one stadium Judd looked out over the sea of people and noticed smoke rising in the distance.

"That is our volcano," an interpreter said. "But don't be alarmed. It has not been active for years. It is only showing off."

People stood in the searing heat to hear Bruce. Muslim leaders in traditional garb stood at the back of the service. At the end of one message, the men tore their robes, cried out, and ran to the front of the stadium.

Judd rushed to Bruce. "Get out of here! They're going to kill you!"

"Wait," Bruce said. "Look."

The men were on their knees, crying out to God. Judd was amazed at what a simple message could do. People were hungry for God.

Bruce spoke freely of the judgments to come. He urged people to accept God's forgiveness before it was too late. He also taught how to start home churches for when public meetings would be outlawed.

Judd missed his friends and was torn by what he felt for Vicki. Bruce kept him busy with many E-mail messages from around the world. With Bruce's help Judd typed answers.

"You have a question here from Rayford about the fifth and seventh?" Judd said. "What does that mean?"

"He's talking about the judgments predicted in Revelation," Bruce said. "We have to be careful. The GC could intercept these, and Rayford would be in danger."

"What are those judgments?"

"Many are clear, but the fifth and seventh are difficult. In his vision, the apostle John sees under the altar in heaven the souls of those who had been slain for the Word of God and for their testimonies. They ask God how long it will be until he avenges their deaths. He gives them white robes and tells them others will be martyred first. So the fifth Seal Judgment costs people who have become believers since the Rapture their lives."

"That could include you or me."

"Any of us," Bruce said.

"What about the seventh?"

"That's a mystery. It's so awesome that when it's revealed in heaven, there is silence for half an hour. Whatever it is, it seems to progress from the sixth seal, which is the greatest earthquake in history, and brings in more judgments, each worse than the one before it."

Judd tried to list the other judgments. "A world war, famine, martyrdom—"

"Don't forget plagues and the death of a quarter of the earth's population," Bruce said as he replied to Rayford's message.

Judd looked over Bruce's shoulder as he typed: "He who dwells in the secret place of the Most High shall abide under the shadow of the Almighty."

Vicki and Chaya followed Bruce and Judd's travels on a world map. A red pin marked each place the two visited.

Judd also uploaded pictures of crowds and interesting sights from each place. In one picture Bruce and Judd wore nervous smiles as they sat at a dinner table. In front of them was an overflowing dish of what looked like small biscuits. Judd held one up and winked at the camera.

"What were those things you were holding in the picture?" Vicki wrote.

"A delicacy," he wrote back. "Sheep's eye-balls."

Chaya gagged and Vicki wrote, "You actually ate those things!?"

"It would have been impolite not to," Judd said. "For sheep's eyeballs they weren't bad."

Chaya answered the door as Judd wrote Vicki their schedule. "Bruce and I are having lunch with some important people who just had to see us, and then we're heading home. Can't wait to see you."

Just then Chaya stepped back from the door and gasped. "Mother!"

*

The waitress spoke in broken English. "Man in corner buy meal for you, mister sir."

Bruce and Judd looked, but there was no one to thank. Bruce shrugged and turned back to the several guests at his table.

"Doctor Barnes," the interpreter at the table said.

"Please," Bruce said. "Call me pastor. I'm not a doctor."

"Yes, pastor," the man said. "The others want me to thank you for teaching us. But they ask, what do they do now? Many thousands have believed your message."

"Get your people into the Bible," Bruce said. The interpreter rattled off the translation. "Study the Scriptures daily. Nothing is more important. We must be ready for the return of Christ."

On the plane that night, Bruce sat next to a businessman from Chicago. Judd closed his eyes and leaned against the window as he listened to Bruce describe what had happened to him during the disappearances.

"That might be good for you," the man said, "but your faith is too exclusive, saying there is only one way to God. Enigma Babylon says all paths to God are valid. Just like there are a lot of planes you could take to Chicago."

"It's true that the message of the Bible is different from Enigma Babylon," Bruce said. "Let me show you."

Judd drifted off as he heard Bruce's Bible pages turning. He awoke to shouting.

"Somebody do something!"

"What's wrong with him?"

"Is he dead?"

Bruce slumped in the aisle. A flight attendant rushed to him.

"He didn't look good, and I told him so," the man said. "Then he just passed out."

"We should be in Chicago in two hours," the attendant said.

"He looks pretty bad," the man said. "Can't you do anything?"

Judd unbuckled and leaned over Bruce's body.

Bruce's color wasn't right. His lips moved. Judd leaned closer.

"Give it to him," Bruce managed.

"Give who what, Bruce?"

"My Bible," Bruce whispered. "Let him read it for himself."

"Excuse me, I'm a doctor," a woman said, and the aisle cleared.

TEN

The Shepherd's Fall

MRS. Stein had changed since Vicki last saw her. Her eyes had dark circles, her hair had thinned, and she looked tired. Chaya invited her in, and Vicki excused herself.

"No," Mrs. Stein said. "I'd like you to stay if Chaya doesn't mind."

The three sat in the living room in strained silence until Mrs. Stein spoke. "I've come to the point where I don't care what your father thinks. He told me not to come. He said seeing you would just upset me more."

"What's wrong, Mom?"

"I had a routine checkup," Mrs. Stein said. "But the doctor found a lump. He said it was likely nothing to worry about." Her eyes were vacant, and her chin trembled. "It wasn't routine. I have cancer."

She broke down. Chaya put her arm around her mother. "I had no idea," she said. "I'm here for you, Mom."

By the time the plane landed in Chicago
Bruce was sitting up and feeling better.
The man beside him would not take Bruce's
Bible, but Judd got his business card
and promised to send one from Ryan's
stash.

Loretta, the church secretary, met them at
the airport and was upset about Bruce's
condition. "I'm taking you straight to the
emergency room."

"Nonsense," Bruce said. "I'm fine. I need
to get back to the church. If I'm not feeling
better tomorrow, I'll see a doctor."

After debriefing at home, Judd learned from
John the latest about Mark.

"Three more militia exercises in the last
week," John said. "They're gearing up for
something. Mark won't talk specifics, but he
called our relatives who live near Washington, D.C. and told them to leave and stay out
of major East Coast cities."

"But if Bruce is right," Judd said. "The
uprising against the Antichrist will be crushed.
And if Mark gets involved, he doesn't have a
chance."

❋

"Your father has been telling me to forget about you," Mrs. Stein said. "But I can't. Plus I'm scared, and I feel something is missing in my life."

"God loves you, Mom. He can give you peace. You can know that your sins are forgiven and that you'll spend eternity with him."

"You can't know!" Mrs. Stein said. "It is arrogant to say such a thing."

Vicki grabbed a Bible, and Chaya read from the book of John. "And truly Jesus did many other signs in the presence of His disciples, which are not written in this book; but these are written that you may believe that Jesus is the Christ, the Son of God, and that believing you may have life in His name."

"This is what Rabbi Ben-Judah was talking about on TV," Mrs. Stein said.

"Exactly," Chaya said. "It's what I discovered. We Jewish people have been looking for Messiah. But he has already come."

"If your father knew I was talking to you—"

"You said you didn't care what Dad thinks," Chaya said. "Please, Mom, let me show you more."

Vicki made lunch while the two talked. Chaya told her mother about her friend at the University of Chicago who had explained who Jesus was and what he had done. At times Mrs. Stein argued, but each time Chaya gently led her back to the Bible.

Before they ate, Vicki thanked God for Mrs. Stein and prayed for her upcoming surgery. "Give her the peace that passes all understanding."

When she looked up, Mrs. Stein was crying.

꙳

When Judd called Bruce later that afternoon to tell him about Mark, Bruce sounded weak. "You OK?" Judd said.

"I can't talk long," Bruce said. "But don't worry. I'll be all right. And so will Mark. He has to make his own decisions."

꙳

Mrs. Stein thanked Vicki and gathered her things. Her surgery was set for Friday morning at Northwest Community Hospital. "Don't come to see me until the next morning."

"Dad can't keep me from seeing you."

"Please," Mrs. Stein said, "we can talk Saturday."

"Mom, don't go into surgery without settling this."

"That is between God and me. I will take it up with him in my own time."

❋

Judd and John met secretly with Vicki and Chaya late the next night, and they brought each other up to date.

"Mark's ready to give his life for the militia," John said.

"When a person is that committed," Judd said, "there's no way to stop him."

"Tie him up and stick him in the basement," Vicki said.

Judd laughed.

"I'm serious," she said. "Give him something that puts him to sleep, and lock him up till this blows over."

"And how long are you going to keep him?" Judd said. "He'll never trust us again."

"We'd only be doing it because we care," Vicki said.

"And if it works, we use it as a new evangelism tool," John said. "Lock all non-Christians in Bruce's basement 'til they see the light."

Vicki said, "He's your cousin! I'd think you'd care more about him than that."

John stared at her. "I do care. I want to knock some sense into him, and I'd do it if I could. He's bigger than me, and all that training has made him hard as a rock."

"Have you thought about going to the authorities?" Chaya said. "I know it's drastic, but if they know about it beforehand, they can stop it, and no one gets hurt."

"I couldn't think of giving him over to the Global Community goons," John said.

Judd had been quiet. "If the militia is really planning a strike against the Global Community," he said, "one of their targets has to be Nicolae Carpathia."

"Of course," John said. "They wouldn't be able to restore President Fitzhugh if they don't take him out."

"Which puts whose life in danger?" Judd said.

"Rayford Steele's!" Vicki gasped.

"Bingo," Judd said. "Maybe Mrs. Steele's, too. I wonder if that would change Mark's mind?"

"It wouldn't," Mark said, and everyone jerked to attention. "Hi, everybody. Thanks for inviting me."

Judd didn't know what to say. John stared at the floor.

"I don't want anyone to die, and I don't want to die. Captain Steele knew the risks when he took the job.

"Have any of you considered the possibility that I'm right? I'm going to fight the enemy of this country and the enemy of our souls. People are going to die no matter what. You ought to support me and be thankful the militia is willing to put it all on the line."

"Nobody questions your motives," Judd said. "We just don't want you to throw your life away."

Chaya said, "Isn't Scripture clear that no uprising will stop the Antichrist?"

Mark shrugged. "That's your interpretation," he said. "If God calls you to do something, you've got to do it no matter what other people say. I thought you'd be behind me. If you can't support me, fine. But don't get in my way."

The phone rang, and Vicki handed it to Judd. It was Loretta. When he laid the phone down he felt sick to his stomach.

"What is it?" Vicki said.

Loretta found Pastor Bruce on the floor of his study," Judd said. "They're taking him to the emergency room!"

Judd raced to Northwest Community Hospital in Arlington Heights. He found Loretta with an elder from New Hope Village Church.

"Bruce was disoriented," Loretta said nervously. "He didn't want us to bring him, but he looked so pale."

Eventually a doctor told them, "We're going to monitor him here tonight. His heart rate is erratic, but he's resting. Could be a heart attack, or he may have picked up something overseas. You can see him if you make it quick."

Judd was shocked to find Bruce hooked up to tubes and monitors. Judd took Bruce's hand, which was limp and unusually cold.

Bruce's eyelids fluttered. He whispered, "So tired. I wanted to surprise them Saturday."

"Surprise who?" Judd said, but Bruce didn't respond.

Bruce's Bible lay on the stand by the bed. Judd opened it to one of Bruce's favorite passages, and his voice broke as he leaned close. "He who dwells in the secret place of the Most High shall abide under the shadow of the Almighty."

ELEVEN

Death Strike

"STOP treating us like little kids," Lionel said at breakfast Friday morning. "It's not right to have meetings without us."

Ryan was furious. "Mark is our friend, too," he said. "We've got a right to know what's going on."

"I was afraid you'd want to follow him," Judd said. "What was I supposed to do?"

"Let us go see Bruce then."

"Can't. Sorry."

"See," Ryan said. "This is the same thing."

"They won't let you in," Judd said. "Maybe when he's feeling better."

"I'm going to send him a card," Ryan muttered as he slammed the door.

Judd called Loretta for the latest on Bruce. She said, "He rested through the night and told me he wants to be out in time to meet Rayford and the rest tomorrow."

"So that's what he meant about meeting people for lunch," Judd said. "Is Captain Steele flying Carpathia into the country?"

"I don't have a clue."

Vicki drove Chaya to the hospital Friday morning and saw Chaya's mother and father walk in. Chaya left a bouquet of flowers at the front desk for her mother. They asked about Bruce, but the nurses were tight-lipped.

Patricia Devlin, the head nurse, said, "Family members?"

Vicki said, "Daughter."

"No change," the nurse said. "Check back later."

"I can't even see my own father?"

Ms. Devlin peered at Vicki over her glasses. "You look a little old to be his daughter," she said. "But anyway, his doctor says no visitors until his illness is identified."

John and Mark were at Judd's that evening when Ryan handed Judd a card with a beautiful picture of clouds on the front.

"It's for Bruce," Ryan said. "I hope he likes it."

"I'm sure he will," Judd said, "but I can't promise when he'll get it."

"Then I'll take it to him myself."

"You can't," Judd said. "I told you that."

Judd answered the phone, and a mysterious voice asked for Mark.

When Mark took it, he said, "We are? When? Where? I'll be there."

"Hey, I got a hot date I forgot about," Mark said. Judd and John didn't smile. "Can you give John a ride home?"

Judd nodded.

Mark paused at the door. "You guys take care of yourselves, OK?"

⁂

The phone woke Vicki Saturday morning. Judd was frantic.

"I need your help," Judd said. "Ryan isn't in his room. He's gone."

"Where could he be?"

"He talked about going to see Bruce."

"That's a long way on busy streets," Vicki said. "What can I do?"

"Come help me look for him," Judd said.

"Will do. Chaya and I are heading to the hospital to check on her mom, anyway," Vicki said. "We'll look for him there. How's Bruce?"

"Loretta says he called for his laptop, which was good news, but then she found out they were moving him to Intensive Care. She thinks he had a premonition."

"A premonition?" Vicki said. "About what? He's not that sick, is he?"

"I don't know," Judd said. "Bruce asked her to print out everything from his hard drive."

"By the way," Judd added quickly, "John said Mark didn't come home last night."

Ryan pedaled faster. He hated shutting Phoenix up at the house, but there was no way he could take him. He wanted to stay on less crowded streets, but to get his bearings he had to follow the main roads.

He asked directions several times and was relieved when a woman told him to cut through her yard. The hospital was on the other side of a grassy knoll.

Ryan parked his bike and locked it to a post near the emergency room entrance. Finding the hospital was the easy part. The hard part would be making it to Bruce's room.

An older woman at the information desk told him Bruce was on the fourth floor in Intensive Care. "But you won't be able to go up there, son."

Ryan waited until the elevator was empty, pushed the button for the fourth floor, then hit floor five as well.

On the fourth floor Ryan saw the nurses' station and noticed three nurses pushing a man in a wheelchair. The doors closed, and Ryan rode up to five.

From there he hurried to the stairway, walked down one flight, and watched the nurses through the small window.

When everyone seemed busy he opened the door and slipped down the hall. He found Bruce's room and made sure no one was watching as he entered.

Ryan wasn't sure it was Bruce, there were so many machines and tubes hooked up to him. When he finally saw his face, Ryan knew.

"I brought you something," Ryan said softly.

Ryan held the card in front of Bruce's closed eyes. "It looks like heaven, or at least what I think heaven might look like," Ryan said.

He heard voices and a cart outside. Ryan hit the floor and rolled under the bed as someone entered, took something, and left.

Ryan rolled out from under the bed. He touched Bruce's face. "If it hadn't been for you," he whispered, "I don't know what would have happened to me."

Ryan pulled up a chair, sat, and laid his head on the bed beside Bruce.

Ryan felt something on his shoulder and flinched. He was afraid someone had discovered him. But it was Bruce's hand, barely moving, patting Ryan's shoulder.

※

Loretta was ashen when Judd found her at the church. She sat alone, staring at the computer as the printer worked away.

"That young man taught me more about the Bible than I learned in all my years of Sunday school," she said.

"What's happened?" Judd said.

"I just got off the phone with the hospital. Bruce has slipped into a coma."

※

Vicki saw no sign of Ryan. Chaya's mother came through surgery, but they wouldn't know for a few days if the last-ditch effort was successful. Chaya visited her mother, while Vicki headed for Intensive Care.

Vicki briskly walked past the nurses' station, hoping she could find Bruce's room quickly and ask him if Ryan had been there.

The writing was poor on the clipboards on

each door. Vicki bent close to read, when the
door opened and an orderly nearly knocked
her over.

He eyed Vicki suspiciously. "This is Intensive Care. You shouldn't be here."

"Is this Pastor Barnes's room?" Vicki said.

"It is, but . . . "

"I'm his daughter."

"You're Vicki?" he said.

"You know my name?"

"Pastor Bruce told me about you before he
slipped into a coma."

Vicki gasped.

He pulled her inside the room and shut
the door. "I'm sorry. I assumed you knew."

Vicki heard the beep of the monitors
fastened to Bruce's chest. Tubes ran everywhere, and an oxygen mask covered his
face.

"What did he say?" Vicki said, choking
back tears.

"First thing he wanted to know was if I
knew Jesus. He was in and out after that.
Might have been dreaming. Mumbled something about a wedding."

Vicki nodded.

"He opened his eyes and asked me if I was
Vicki. I said I didn't know who Vicki was, but
I sure hoped she didn't look like me. He said

you were his only daughter now. Then he went back to sleep. The next time I came in, he was in a coma."

Bruce's Bible lay on the nightstand. Beside it was a card with clouds on the front.

"You'd better get back to the waiting room," the orderly said.

"Wait," Vicki said. "You didn't see a boy up here, did you?"

"No boys in this room. Just doctors and nurses, and me, of course. Now come on."

"One more thing," Vicki said. "How did you answer? Do you know Jesus?"

The orderly smiled. "You're Pastor Bruce's daughter all right."

Vicki met Chaya in the lobby.

"Mother actually had a Bible open," Chaya said. "But she was afraid Dad would walk in."

Vicki asked at the front desk, but no one had seen a boy on a bike. As she and Chaya were getting into the car, a plane flew low over the parking lot.

Seconds later, a huge explosion erupted.

＊

Judd felt the earth shudder at the church before the loud rumble. Windowpanes crashed in the back. From the parking lot he saw black smoke rise in the distance and bombers from all directions. Another explosion, then a bigger one, hurtled plumes of smoke high into the air.

He jumped in his car and headed toward the hospital. He dialed his house on his cell phone. Lionel answered.

"Any sign of Ryan?" Judd said.

"Not yet. Did you hear that noise?"

"I heard it. Take cover in the basement."

Fire trucks, ambulances, and police cruisers swirled around Judd. The radio gave the sports report, then the weather.

"Come on, come on, what happened?" Judd said.

Finally a voice interrupted. "This breaking story! An explosion in northwest suburban Arlington Heights. We have a reporter on the way. Wait, excuse me. I'm told we have a woman on the phone who's at the scene. Hello? Ma'am?"

"There were planes and then *kaboom!*"

"Planes? This was some kind of an attack?"

"An attack. That's exactly what it was."

"And where are you?"

"Near the old racecourse off Euclid," she said. "They're still comin' in and droppin' their bombs."

"Don't you know the target?"

"No, but it was south of me. I can see the smoke from my front window."

Judd saw the same mushroom cloud and then the fire. Traffic stopped. He parked and took off on foot. He called Lionel again. Still no sign of Ryan.

Judd called the hospital but couldn't get through. He could smell the acrid smoke and feel the heat. Fire trucks and ambulances sat in the middle of the street. He dialed Vicki at home. No answer.

Running, he saw a boy on a bicycle. "Any other kids come by here?" Judd yelled.

"No," the kid said. "And stay away from the hospital. It's like a war zone."

"They're taking the wounded there?"

"It was hit!" the kid said. He rode away, pale and clearly terrified.

Judd's head spun, and the smoke made it difficult to breathe. He cut through a parking lot, then past a grassy area. Judd's heart sank as he came over the rise and saw the hospital. Part of the full height of the structure was still intact, but much of it was rubble. A few white-uniformed workers scurried about.

He heard a plane directly overhead and looked up in time to see it deliver its payload. The bomb wobbled in the air, then straightened out. The plane veered off with a deafening roar as Judd hit the ground and covered his head.

The earth shook with the force of the explosion. No more planes. Only sirens and the crackling fire and the sobs.

And the sobs were his own.

TWELVE

The Search

As THE smoke cleared Judd ran full tilt toward the hospital. Police and firemen were just arriving. Bodies lay scattered. He heard the faint cry of a newborn in the rubble, and four officers began lifting concrete.

Judd couldn't believe anyone could have survived. Part of the structure looked normal, but the other half looked like a mashed toy. Girders protruded. Water sprayed from broken pipes. Hospital equipment lay charred and twisted on the ground.

Bruce was in there somewhere. Judd had to find him. As more emergency personnel arrived, Judd acted like he was supposed to be there. He kept his head down and walked toward what used to be the Intensive Care unit.

Vicki and Chaya were just pulling away when the first plane struck. They ran through the parking lot and into backyards. As planes roared overhead, Vicki and Chaya jumped fences and ran around swimming pools.

Just when they thought they were far enough away, a terrific blast shook the earth. Streetlights shattered, and houses exploded a block away. With fire and falling debris around them, they kept going, dodging cars that had run off the road. People screamed in terror as the planes kept coming.

Vicki and Chaya sprinted ten minutes until a woman called out to them from her house. She took the girls to her basement, where they listened to the thunder overhead.

"Who would attack us?" the woman said. She turned on the television. The Cable News Network/Global Community Network correspondent was broadcasting live just outside Washington, D.C.

"The fate of Global Community Potentate Nicolae Carpathia remains in question at this hour as Washington lies in ruins. The massive assault was launched by East Coast militia, with the aid of the United States of Britain and the former sovereign state of Egypt, not part of the Middle Eastern Commonwealth."

Chaya shook her head. The once beautiful view of Washington, D.C. was now a disaster area.

"Potentate Carpathia arrived here last night and was thought to be staying in the presidential suite of the Capital Noir, but eyewitnesses say that the luxury hotel was leveled this morning.

"Global Community peacekeeping forces immediately retaliated and have attacked a former Nike base in suburban Chicago."

"What's a Nike base?" Vicki said.

"That old building near the hospital," the woman said. "Nike is a type of missile. They had training fields over there, barracks, lots of jeeps. But it's been closed for years. People say the militia was using it."

The report switched to Chicago. A man at a news desk stammered through the information.

"Uh, we have reports of civilian casualties in the surrounding suburbs, and uh, a colossal traffic tie-up is hampering rescue efforts. Please, if you are anywhere near the suburbs of Arlington Heights, Prospect Heights, Mount Prospect, or Rolling Meadows, take caution. Find a safe place for you and your family.

"Here's what we know right now about the strike on the Nike base. We are told that

Global Community intelligence has uncovered a plot to destroy Potentate Carpathia's plane at O'Hare."

"Mr. Steele!" Vicki said.

"The attack on the Nike base was effected without nuclear weapons," the man continued. "Again, *without* the use of nuclear weapons. A statement from Global Community command says there is no danger of radiation fallout in the Chicago area."

The station switched to a network reporter. "Egyptian ground forces moving toward Iraq have been wiped out by Global Community air forces, thwarting an obvious siege upon New Babylon. Global Community forces are now advancing on England. Ah, please stand by. . . . Potentate Carpathia is safe! He will address the nation in a few moments."

Judd's cell phone rang.

"Judd, it's John." He sounded awful. "I think Mark was at the Nike base."

"Oh, no!" Judd said. "The hospital was hit, too."

"I'm a few blocks away," John said. "I'll meet you there."

To Vicki, Nicolae Carpathia sounded calm, as if commenting on a golf tournament rather than World War III.

"Loyal citizens of the Global Community," Carpathia said, "I come to you today with a broken heart, unable to tell you even from where I speak. For more than a year we have worked to draw this Global Community together under a banner of peace and harmony. Today, unfortunately, we have been reminded again that there are still those among us who would pull us apart.

"It is no secret that I am, always have been, and always will be a pacifist. I do not believe in war. I do not believe in weaponry. I do not believe in bloodshed. On the other hand, I feel responsible for you, my brother or my sister in this global village.

"Global Community peacekeeping forces have already crushed the resistance. The death of innocent civilians weighs heavy on me, but I pledge immediate judgment upon all enemies of peace. The beautiful capital of the United States of North America has been laid waste, and you will hear stories of more destruction and death. Our goal remains peace and reconstruction. I will be back at the secure headquarters in New Babylon in due time and will communicate with you frequently.

"Above all, do not fear. Live in confidence that no threat to global tranquility will be tolerated, and no enemy of peace will survive."

A correspondent for CNN/GCN recapped Carpathia's statement. "And this late word: Anti-Global Community militia forces have threatened nuclear war on New York City, primarily Kennedy International Airport. Civilians are fleeing the area.

"And now this from London," he said, touching his hand to his forehead. "I'm sorry. A one-hundred-megaton bomb has destroyed Heathrow Airport, and radiation fallout is threatening the area for miles."

"It's the end of the world," the woman said to Vicki and Chaya.

Judd avoided eye contact with the growing number of police and emergency workers. He saw several people lifting bodies to a makeshift outdoor morgue.

"We're getting a patient list and an employee record from the office," Judd heard a man say to rescue workers. "When we get it, we need to reconcile that list with the ID bracelets."

"Any survivors?" another man asked.

"Three women," the man said. "Two

nurses and a doctor. They were outside for a smoke when the bombing started."

The men scattered. Judd looked at the row of lifeless bodies. He went to the first and slowly lifted the white sheet. A woman. *Who was she?* Judd wondered.

Next was a young bald man, probably a cancer patient. The third was an elderly man with white hair.

Judd stood over the fourth body and heard the workers returning. He lifted the sheet and gasped.

Vicki and Chaya waited until they were sure the bombing had stopped. The lady begged them to stay.

"My mother was at the hospital," Chaya said. "And Vicki's father. We have to go back."

By the time they reached the hospital, police barrier tape had been stretched around the campus. Guards patrolled the area.

Chaya pointed excitedly toward the debris. "It's Judd," she said.

They both yelled at him and waved as Judd was led from the area by two guards. As he got closer, Vicki could see Judd crying.

He ducked under the police tape and fell to his knees. "I saw him, Vick'."

"Who?" Vicki said. "Ryan?"

"Bruce. They just brought him out and laid him in the grass." Judd looked up at Vicki. "Bruce is gone. Dead."

Vicki and Chaya burst into tears and embraced Judd. Why would God take Bruce now? Vicki shook. The man who had taken her in, who had given so much to teach them the truth of God's Word, had fallen.

"My mother," Chaya said. "How will I find out about my mother?"

"They're identifying bodies," Judd said. He suggested they stay while he went to find John at the Nike base. They would try to find Mark. Judd left Vicki his cell phone and asked her to keep in touch with Lionel.

※

Judd met John near the Nike base. Smoke rose from the building and small explosions still erupted inside. Judd approached an officer. "What happened?"

"Global Community took out the militia," the officer said. "Their stash of weapons is blowing up now."

"Any survivors?" John said.

The officer raised his eyebrows and shook his head. "In there? Anybody who survived the bombs would have been vaporized by the heat."

John hung his head.

"Don't give up," Judd said. "You never know."

They jogged toward Judd's car. Traffic was backed up as far as he could see.

"Cut down this alley," John said. "There's a convenience store down here Mark talked about. The owner might know something."

When they pulled off the street, Judd noticed Mark's truck parked in the back.

John ran toward the vehicle. He skidded to a stop and peered through the window. Judd fell in behind him. On the seat of the truck, flat on his face, lay Mark.

"Oh no," John said.

When Judd opened the door, Mark sat up. He wore his battle fatigues, and his face was painted green and black.

"Don't say it," Mark said. "You were right."

"Are you OK?" John said.

"They're all gone," Mark said.

"How did you make it out?" Judd said.

"Major Evers sent the younger guys out just before the attack. He must have known."

"Come on," John said. "This area will be crawling with GC in a few minutes. Come back for the truck later."

Judd brought his car around and hustled Mark into the trunk.

Tears were Vicki's first response to Bruce's death. The more she thought of him, the more she felt like she had been kicked in the stomach. There were no words for the pain. Bruce had never asked to be called "Dad" or "Father," but in many ways she felt closer to him than to her real dad. Now Bruce was gone, and she wanted to scream. At the same time she was overcome by a stillness and a peace she couldn't explain.

After a few minutes she realized there was more to do. *Ryan,* she thought. Vicki called Lionel, but there was still no sign of him. She and Chaya held each other and wept as they waited for word about her mother. Suddenly Vicki spotted Chaya's father running toward the morgue area. Officials shooed him away. He stood behind the yellow tape and stared at the ground.

A nurse finally led Chaya toward the temporary morgue. Vicki watched as Mr. Stein ran to Chaya. The nurse checked her clipboard and led them stiffly away. Vicki saw Chaya look at her father, but it appeared he did not return her glance.

Vicki thought about Bruce. He had treated her like she was his own, and now he was gone. *Gone.* When Vicki allowed that thought, she staggered. The pain cut so deep, it was almost unbearable. There would be a time of grieving, she knew. Now she had to concentrate.

Vicki called Lionel. "Ryan?" she said.

"His bike is gone," Lionel said. "And he left Phoenix."

Chaya returned without her father, beaming through her tears.

※

Judd weaved through traffic and onto side streets. He had to get Mark to safety before the GC resumed their search. Judd saw a roadblock and turned down another side street. Global Community peacekeepers were scouring each car.

After nearly an hour, Judd pulled into his garage. Mark was exhausted. He tore off his fatigues and ran past Lionel for the shower. Judd found him a change of clothes.

"Vicki said Chaya identified her mom's body," Lionel said.

Judd slumped into a kitchen chair.

※

Chaya put her head on Vicki's shoulder and wept.

"I'm so sorry," Vicki said.

"She looked so beautiful."

"How is your father?"

Chaya shook her head. She held up a crumpled piece of paper, the note she had given her mother that morning.

"Mom always wrote everything down," Chaya said. "We'd find notes all over the house."

Chaya turned the paper over, and Vicki saw Mrs. Stein's handwriting.

"Forgive me, God. Help me live for you and for your Son, Jesus, the Messiah."

Everybody met at Judd's house that evening, and he stood before pale, frightened faces. What would they do without Bruce? How would they find Ryan? And would they have to face further conflict in the future?

"This is a terrible day," he said. "And we have to face the fact that Ryan may have been—"

"Don't write him off yet," Lionel said, his voice quavering. "He's tough."

"Bruce said once that one of the hardest things you ever have to do is let go of someone you care about," Judd said.

"I'm telling you, don't count him out!" Lionel sobbed.

"I'm sorry," Judd said. "All we can do is try

to stay safe and honor the memory of our friends by telling everybody the truth about God, no matter what the cost, no matter what anybody does."

"I'm in," John said.

"Me, too," Chaya whispered.

Vicki nodded, and Mark cleared his throat. "I want to fight the enemy," he said. "This time, I want to do it the right way."

Lionel rose and moved slowly toward the stairs.

"Lionel?" Vicki said, worried as much about him as about how she was going to cope with fresh grief.

He turned. "You all can rah-rah about the future, and yeah, you can count me in. But don't include me in cryin' over Ryan, 'cause I'm not buying that yet. He'll be back."

About the Authors

Jerry B. Jenkins (www.jerryjenkins.com) is the writer of the Left Behind series. He is author of more than one hundred books, of which six have reached the *New York Times* best-seller list. Former vice president for publishing for the Moody Bible Institute of Chicago, he also served many years as editor of *Moody* magazine and is now Moody's writer-at-large.

His writing has appeared in publications as varied as *Reader's Digest, Parade,* in-flight magazines, and many Christian periodicals. He has written books in four genres: biography, marriage and family, fiction for children, and fiction for adults.

Jenkins's biographies include books with Hank Aaron, Bill Gaither, Luis Palau, Walter Payton, Orel Hershiser, Nolan Ryan, Brett Butler, and Billy Graham, among many others.

Six of his apocalyptic novels—*Left Behind, Tribulation Force, Nicolae, Soul Harvest, Apollyon,* and *Assassins*—have appeared on the Christian Booksellers Association's best-selling fiction list and the *Publishers Weekly* religion best-seller list. *Left Behind* was nominated for Book of the Year by the Evangelical Christian Publishers Association in 1997, 1998, and 1999.

As a marriage and family author and speaker, Jenkins has been a frequent guest on Dr. James Dobson's *Focus on the Family* radio program.

Jerry is also the writer of the nationally syndicated sports story comic strip *Gil Thorp,* distributed to newspapers across the United States by Tribune Media Services.

Jerry and his wife, Dianna, live in Colorado.

Limited speaking engagement information available through speaking@jerryjenkins.com.

Dr. Tim LaHaye (www.timlahayeministries.org), who conceived the idea of fictionalizing an account of the Rapture and the Tribulation, is a noted author, minister, educator, and nationally recognized speaker on Bible prophecy. He presides over Tim LaHaye Ministries and is chairman and founder of the Pre-Trib Research Center. Presently Dr. LaHaye speaks at many of the major Bible prophecy conferences in the U.S. and Canada, where his eight current prophecy books are very popular.

Dr. LaHaye is a graduate of Bob Jones University and holds the D.Min. from Western Theological Seminary and the Lit.D. from Liberty University. For twenty-five years he pastored one of the nation's outstanding churches in San Diego, which grew to three locations. It was during that time that he founded two accredited Christian high schools, a Christian school system of ten schools, and Christian Heritage College.

Dr. LaHaye has written over forty books, with over 22 million copies in print in thirty-two languages. He has written books on a wide variety of subjects, such as family life, temperaments, and Bible prophecy. His current fiction works, written by Jerry Jenkins—*Left Behind, Tribulation Force, Nicolae, Soul Harvest, Apollyon,* and *Assassins*—have all reached number one on the Christian best-seller charts. Other works by Dr. LaHaye are *Spirit-Controlled Temperament; How to Be Happy though Married; The Act of Marriage; Revelation Unveiled; Understanding the Last Days; Rapture under Attack: Will You Escape the Tribulation?; Are We Living in the End Times?;* and the youth fiction series Left Behind: The Kids.

He is the father of four children and grandfather of nine. Snow skiing, waterskiing, motorcycling, golfing, vacationing with family, and jogging are among his leisure activities.

The Future Is Clear

In one shocking moment, millions around the globe disappear. Those left behind face an uncertain future—especially the four kids who now find themselves alone.

Best-selling authors Jerry B. Jenkins and Tim LaHaye present the Rapture and Tribulation through the eyes of four friends—Judd, Vicki, Lionel, and Ryan. As the world falls in around them, they band together to find faith and fight the evil forces that threaten their lives.

#1: The Vanishings Four friends face Earth's last days together.

#2: Second Chance The kids search for the truth.

#3: Through the Flames The kids risk their lives.

#4: Facing the Future The kids prepare for battle.

#5: Nicolae High The Young Trib Force goes back to school.

#6: The Underground The Young Trib Force fights back.

#7: Busted! The Young Trib Force faces pressure.

#8: Death Strike The Young Trib Force faces war.

BOOKS #9 AND #10 COMING SOON!